There I Find Wisdom
Strawberry Sands Book Nine

Jessie Gussman

Published By: Jessie Gussman

Contents

Acknowledgements

Cover art by Kim Killion of The Killion Group
Editing by Heather Hayden
Narration by Jay Dyess
Author Services by CE Author Assistant

Listen to the unabridged audio for FREE performed by Jay Dyess on the Say with Jay channel on YouTube. Get early access to all of Jay's recordings and listen to Jessie's books before they're available to the general public, plus get daily Bible readings by Jay and bonus scenes by becoming a Say with Jay channel member .

Chapter 1

"Lord, I don't know what I'm going to do."

Dakota Estenben stayed on her knees beside the bed of her grandmother. It was one o'clock in the morning, or somewhere thereabouts. No sound permeated the house, except for her grandmother's breathing, and for all intents and purposes, she was alone.

Her children, at six and eight years of age, were too young to understand that this would be the last night their great-grandmother was with them on earth. Maybe they weren't too young to understand, but they were too young to keep an all-night vigil.

Dakota had tucked them into bed hours ago, knowing they probably wouldn't have a grandmother in the morning.

Or a place to stay.

They wouldn't be out that fast, but it was coming.

Dakota's sister, Kylie, was set to inherit the house.

Dakota had nothing. Not since her divorce, where her husband basically took everything she had.

Yellowstone Gold, her golden Palomino whom she called Goldie, was all Dakota had left in the world, other than a run-down store her grandmother would leave for her once she passed. In order for her to make ends meet, she was going to have to sell Goldie. She loved her horse, but she couldn't allow her children to starve.

She didn't regret her children, but she did regret her marriage.

But she had learned, over the years, that she couldn't live with regrets.

"Kota?"

Her gram's husky voice slid through Dakota's thoughts, and she squeezed the hand she held, lifting her head and peering through the darkness toward the head of the bed.

"Gram?"

Gram had been asleep the entire day before. She hadn't eaten or drunk anything in two days. Dakota had been putting chapstick on her lips to keep them from drying out, but her grandma had refused all ice chips or even a sip of water.

The hospice nurse had said it wouldn't be long.

"Don't forget about the gift shop."

How could she forget?

They knew the contents of the will. Her sister had been given the house. She had been given a worthless, run-down, out-of-business gift shop, with no inventory, in a nowhere town called Strawberry Sands.

It wasn't that she was so upset about it, or that she felt like it was unfair. She didn't expect her gram to give her anything, and she appreciated the fact that her gram felt like she had divided her assets equally between Kylie and Dakota.

The issue was, Dakota couldn't do anything with the gift shop. She wasn't a shopkeeper. She had no desire to live in Michigan. Even if it was a picturesque town beside the lake.

She loved her home in Iowa, such as it was. Since she'd lived with her gram since her divorce.

"Kota," her grandma prompted, unable to get her full name out.

"I won't. I promise, Gram," she said automatically. She wasn't going to forget about it, she just wasn't going to do anything with it. Except... Except she needed to do something.

She had to have a place to live. Kylie and she got along well, but Kylie was expecting Dakota to move out when she inherited the house. Kylie had just gotten married to a man who had three children, and they were planning on living right here.

They hadn't moved in because Dakota was here, and she had been the one taking care of Gram. Kylie had been decent enough to not kick Dakota out while their gram was dying.

Of course, she didn't exactly have that right, not until Gram breathed her last. Since Gram owned the house and would never make Dakota leave.

"Move there," her gram said weakly.

"Move where?" Dakota asked, blinking and coming back to the present. She wanted to savor every last interaction with her grandmother. Maybe she was wrong. Maybe her gram would last longer than what they thought. But the fact that she hadn't eaten, hadn't drunk, hadn't spoken in two days, and now... Now she was going to talk? Dakota should listen.

"To the souvenir shop. Move there."

"Okay, Gram." She wanted to argue. How was she supposed to live in a shop?

"Live above it," Gram said weakly. "Where you stayed with me in the summer."

Dakota vaguely remembered the shop from visiting during the summer when she was a kid. She'd kind of forgotten that there was an apartment above the shop where her gram lived. She could hardly believe it, since she'd stayed there herself. But she hadn't realized that the apartment was part of the shop. She supposed in her head she had thought that her gram had rented the apartment. Or something.

She hadn't paid much attention to what was going on at the shop, because Strawberry Sands had a riding stable, and she had been as wild and free as she could be on the beach with the horses.

But that thought brought her pain too. Because it reminded her of Ryan Landry.

Ryan, whom she'd asked to marry her and who had turned her down. That was why she had ended up with Gregory, her ex.

But she wasn't going there either. She pushed the bad thoughts aside. She couldn't focus on the things that didn't work out. She had to focus on the things that she could control.

Which felt like very little. Except, she still had Goldie. For now.

She could put Goldie up on social media for sale, and she would sell within the hour. Dakota was confident of that. But Goldie had been the one constant that she'd had since her college days. Goldie had been with her as she became a championship contender, had been her best friend, had been the one that she told everything to, as her world came tumbling down, not twice but three times.

First, when her parents had been killed in a freak rodeo accident, and second when she felt like her only choice was to get married, and then again when her marriage imploded.

"I love you," her gram said weakly.

"Gram, I love you too. I wish you weren't leaving me." Boy, how she ever wished her gram wasn't leaving. It felt like everything in her life that she tried to hold onto had been ripped from her.

Everything except her children and Goldie.

"If I didn't leave, you couldn't move on to what's next. Don't be afraid. You know God has everything under control. Just follow His plan."

It was the most Gram had said to her in over a week, but she wanted to snort. It felt like God's plan for her whole life had been to kick her, then kick her harder. And anytime she tried to get up, He'd kick her again.

That felt like a really great sum of God's plan.

But somehow through all that, she never forgot He loved her. She never doubted it. Even though at times it felt like she should. Like the wise thing to do would be to just throw in the towel and admit that if there was a God, she didn't really want to know Him.

Except for the thought that all the bad things that she had gone through had made her stronger and better, had helped her become the person God wanted her to be, so that she could do what God wanted her to do, and she just couldn't let go of Him.

Maybe He really did have a plan for her.

She wanted to believe that. Sometimes, the things that a person really wanted to believe were the hardest things of all.

But she could hardly move forward with God's plan when she had no money, no place to live, and nothing to fall back on, with her gram leaving her.

Except for Goldie. She had Goldie.

The thought made her almost physically sick, but if she was going to move to Michigan, the only way that was going to happen was if she sold her horse.

As a grand champion barrel racing contender, Goldie was well known on the rodeo circuit, and even though she was past her prime and would not be winning any championships, she would be prized as a broodmare. Which is what Dakota had planned for her, if she'd ever been able to have a place where Goldie could stay.

Currently, she was boarding Goldie and was two months behind on her payments to the stable owner.

The stable owner knew her gram was dying, and had given her grace, but Dakota couldn't promise to pay, because she had no idea how she was even going to feed her children, let alone board her horse.

She had to face the fact that as a responsible mother, it was more important that her children eat than that she keep her horse.

With that thought in her head, and with her gram's hand going limp, Dakota put her forehead back down on her gram's bed, still on her knees, and prayed again, "Lord, I don't want to let her go."

But a peace came to her, and while it wasn't an audible voice, she understood that what she had just thought—selling her horse and moving to Michigan—was the right thing to do.

Why does life have to be so hard, Lord? Are You really asking me to give up Goldie? She's the last thing I have, other than my children.

She needed to be grateful that God wasn't requiring her children.

I've given You everything. Everything except for them.

And Goldie.

She sighed. If she claimed to love God, if she claimed to be a follower of Christ, if she claimed to want God's glory and not her own, then giving up her horse shouldn't be such a struggle. It should be something she gladly did, if it furthered God's plan in her life. It shouldn't be something that was pried out of her cold, resisting fingers.

Gram's breathing changed, becoming harsher, harder, and Dakota lifted her head.

It was a shift that she immediately knew signaled the end.

She grabbed her phone and texted her sister.

Gram is leaving us.

Her sister probably wouldn't come, but she wanted to give her that option. She didn't want to keep her from being with her grandma at the end if she truly wanted to be. Although, they had known for the last several days that any minute could be her last.

And her last words had been to Dakota, telling her to move to Michigan. How could she tell her no? How could she deny her, even if it meant selling her beloved horse?

Her phone buzzed.

Thanks for letting me know. Tell me when she's gone, and I'll call the funeral director.

Dakota stared at her phone. At least Kylie was going to take care of that. They'd already made plans; their gram had even helped. She didn't want a big funeral, didn't want a lot of fanfare, just wanted to be laid to rest as inexpensively as possible without being cremated. Being cremated was too much like going to hell, she said, and she didn't see it in the Bible as a viable thing; it was something that the heathens did. Whether it was or wasn't, they would pay a little extra to give her a traditional burial.

And Kylie would handle it. She would pay for it out of Gram's savings and no doubt pocket the rest.

That was fine with Dakota. She just wished her grandma hadn't needed to go. But God's timing was perfect, and God was calling her home, and there was nothing Dakota could do to stop it.

She held her breath as Gram's breathing became unsteady, rough and loud.

Maybe being on her knees was the proper position, because it was like she could feel the angels coming to carry her grandmother home. Whether they were, whether they weren't, it felt like a sacred thing to be in the presence of someone who stepped from this world into the next.

She held tightly to Gram's hand, knowing that wouldn't keep her, and listened as Gram exhaled. Several dozen seconds later, she inhaled again, and this time, when she breathed out, everything was still.

Dakota let out the breath she had been holding. Just like that, her gram was gone.

And just like that, a new chapter of her life would begin.

Chapter 2

"Yellowstone Gold is for sale."

Ryan Landry held the phone to his ear and stopped in the middle of the sidewalk as he walked down toward the beach in Strawberry Sands.

"Yellowstone Gold?" he repeated, although he had heard his friend Denver loud and clear.

That was Dakota's horse. The one she'd come so close to winning a barrel racing championship on.

Dakota had been a go-get-them kind of girl, and as far as he knew, she'd gotten everything she'd ever set out for. Except for him.

He'd declined her offer of marriage. She was a great friend, and it was possible he had feelings for her, probable, even. He admired her as a barrel racer, but he hadn't wanted to be saddled with a wife and possibly children as he chased his own rodeo dreams. He would never have won the three championships if he'd have married her when she asked.

She hadn't truly loved him or been heartbroken, since the next time he heard about her, she was married with a baby on the way.

That had put the brakes on her rodeo career, and he supposed he should feel like he'd dodged a bullet, but he always felt like maybe she'd been the one who got away, and he'd always regret not going after her.

He didn't know what happened to her, but apparently she and her horse had parted ways, since Yellowstone Gold was up for sale.

"How much?" he asked, rolling over in his mind whether or not he would be able to scrape the money together to get her. He'd been saving to buy property of his own, but using his down payment to buy a horse of Yellowstone Gold's quality would be a wise investment of money that had been meant for a ranch.

Denver mentioned the amount.

"Wow. That's it?"

"The post is five minutes old. If you want her, you better move fast."

"I'll take her. Do whatever you have to to get her. If you can pay for her, I can wire you the money today as soon as the banks open."

He looked at the pink glow on the water. The sun hadn't quite made it up over the eastern horizon, and he was on his way to help his brother feed his horses before he worked with two of the horses he was training in roping and reining.

After that, he would go to the inn to help as a handyman.

He had several ads out with his handyman business, offering services, but he wasn't expecting to get a lot of work here in Strawberry Sands.

Which was just fine by him. The more time he had to work with his horses, the sooner he could sell them, and not just make back the money he'd spent, but hopefully pocket a tiny little profit and put that much more toward his dream of owning his own ranch.

It was almost a dream come true, since he saved his winnings from the rodeo. He'd had endorsements and purse money he'd won, and he was close to being able to afford the ranch of his dreams.

Although it had been hard for him to admit that his rodeo days were over. He didn't want to think that he was getting older, that he would never have another championship belt, never be number one again, never have more accolades to add to his list.

It had taken him a while after he got back to settle into the small-town routine, and humble himself enough to ask the Lord if this was really what God wanted for him, and to give his life over fully to God.

When he was chasing the rodeo circuit, he was sure that was what God wanted him to do. And, as a champion, that gave him a platform to point others to the Lord. But fame was fleeting, and he'd experienced that firsthand. Now, God had other things for him, and he needed to be ready, willing. And he needed to move forward with no regrets, including the fact that Dakota would never be his and he'd most likely missed out on the woman who would have been perfect for him.

"I just messaged the person who posted. She said she was selling for a friend, who had a death in the family and needed to sell ASAP. As soon as I wire the money, she'll take the post down."

"All right. If you don't mind doing it, I'll make sure you're refunded." He couldn't go now, since he was helping his brother, then he needed to help at the inn. Mark Shields had been doing most of the work himself, but he was planting trees today and needed Ryan's help. Ryan had given his word that he would be there.

But he wasn't going to let this opportunity to own Yellowstone Gold pass by. She could be the foundation mare for his entire herd. Any man who'd been on the circuit at all would kill to have her as a part of his herd. The fact that Ryan didn't have any horses currently would make Yellowstone Gold the cornerstone on which he would build everything.

He didn't have to see her to know that she was perfect. Even if she never competed again, and he guessed she wouldn't because she was well past her prime, she was the perfect mare to be put out to pasture and raise babies for him to train.

"I'll let you know if anything changes," Denver said. Then he chuckled. "I figured you'd jump on that."

"I appreciate you thinking of me. Thanks," he said.

They hung up, and Ryan continued down the sidewalk. Whistling a little, excited. He hadn't planned on starting to build his herd this quickly, but he wasn't going to let a chance like this pass by.

With that thought, he grinned and couldn't keep the smile off his face the whole way to his brother Matt's stable.

"Hey there," Matt greeted him as he stepped into the warm, cozy stable where the smell of horse hung heavy in the air.

He would never get tired of that scent, never get tired of the sounds of the stable, the munching of hay, the occasional slurp from a water bucket, or the thump as a hoof hit the wall, whether impatient for its feed or kicking at flies.

"Morning, bro." He paused as Matt looked up at him from where he stood in front of the calendar, writing in a feed ration for their newest horse. His riding stables had been so popular over the last year that he'd added a couple of new horses to his herd, hoping that he could keep up with the bookings of tourists over the coming season.

"Do you have plans for later today?" Ryan asked, figuring there was no point in beating around the bush.

"Nothing aside from making sure the kids get on the bus and moving some hay from the upper barn down here. We're almost out."

"Would you have time to run in to Blueberry Beach to wire money for me?"

"What did you do now?" Matt said, concern lowering his brows but a smile tugging at his lips. Ryan wasn't exactly known as a hothead, but he had done his share of crazy things over the years.

"I'm buying a horse. My buddy's gonna get her for me, and I told him I'd wire him the money today."

"Don't you want to get a vet check?"

"He's got a contract he'll have her sign, and the sale will be contingent on the horse passing a PPE," he said, referencing the prepurchase exam.

"All right. I was concerned you'd gone off the deep end."

"This horse is worth it. Even if she can't do anything but carry babies, she's a once-in-a-lifetime horse, and I'm lucky to be able to get my hands on her."

"I see. I guess in that case, you don't ask too many questions."

"Exactly," Ryan said, glad that Matt got it. Some people would think he was nuts for spending the kind of money that he was going to on a horse. But he knew what she was worth and knew the amount of money that he could make off of her. Not to mention, she was a gorgeous horse with a great personality.

He loved horses, but he was wise enough to know that he couldn't just have horses for the sake of having horses. He didn't have that kind of money. Only people who were born with money or who had a job that enabled them to have money to burn could do that. Ryan had to make money with them if he wanted to be able to continue to have them. And he did. Horses were in his blood.

"Sure. I can head that way."

Ryan felt his phone vibrate and pulled it out of his pocket. "She's already signed the contract."

"What's her name?"

"I'm not sure. She had a friend posting the horse, and Denver is the one who told me. I honestly have no idea. But Denver will make sure all my bases are covered with transferring her papers, and she agreed to my terms, which is that Goldie will pass a PPE and have a negative five panel of course, as well as a negative Coggins."

"Of course."

That was pretty much industry standard. They couldn't ship a horse without a negative Coggins and health certificate. The

PPE went a little further, and the five panel was a typical request.

They settled a few more details, with Denver agreeing to go get the horse, and in five minutes, Ryan shoved his phone back in his pocket.

He just bought a horse.

Part of him was really excited, because he knew the quality of the horse that he'd gotten. But part of him was a little annoyed that he was that much further from owning his own place.

Regardless, maybe something would come up for sale that would be a little less expensive than the places that he'd been looking at. He didn't want to move too far from Strawberry Sands. His entire family was here.

There was a time in his life where he said he'd never go back to his hometown. Never move back home. That time was long gone. After being on the rodeo circuit for as many years as what he had, he'd learned to appreciate the value of family. The way he could depend on his siblings to back him, that he could call them up and they would give him a hand immediately. He didn't have too many people he felt comfortable sharing the bank account with, but he trusted his brother Matt completely.

Matt had bailed him out more than once and helped him when he needed it. He'd needed Matt on his bank account in case he needed something done while he was on the road and couldn't find a branch of his bank in the area he was in.

Back in the old days anyway. Now with Internet banking, he could bank pretty much anywhere. But it didn't used to be like that.

Regardless, he grinned to himself, and got to work, feeding the horses. They chatted while they worked, with Matt eventually saying he could finish up if Ryan wanted to head out.

Ryan thanked him and walked out of the barn, turning and walking up the sand to the sidewalk, thinking about Goldie and his plans for his herd.

He ran into his mother after less than a block.

"Ryan. I've been looking for you."

"You could call me," he said, feeling like that was a reasonable idea.

"Well, I could, but I have something I need to ask you, and I wanted to ask you in person."

That didn't sound good. Anything that couldn't be done over the phone was always something that a person probably didn't want to do. At least in Ryan's experience.

"What's up?" he asked.

"Do you remember the lady who used to own the souvenir shop? She and I were good friends."

"Man. That was years ago. I haven't seen her in...at least a decade, maybe two."

He didn't mention that her granddaughter used to come spend time with her during the summer. Dakota. Funny that he'd just bought a horse that used to belong to Dakota, and now here was his mom talking about Dakota's grandmother.

A lot of times when something like that happened, he figured the Lord was trying to get his attention. But his ship with Dakota had sailed a long time ago. About the time he declined her offer of marriage.

There were a lot of times that he regretted that, but he hadn't been in any position to get married. And he wouldn't have been able to chase the rodeo circuit as long as he had, if he had taken on a wife. Wouldn't have won those championships, had the endorsements, be almost all the way to owning his own ranch.

She'd had a child not long after she got married, and she got married not long after she'd asked him. So she couldn't have been too stuck on him.

That child could have been his.

He pushed the thought aside. He and Dakota had a little bit more history than what most people knew, and maybe that was one of the reasons that he declined her offer. She scared him.

"Right?" his mother said, and he pulled himself out of his contemplation. Dakota seemed to do that to him. Even now, all these years later.

"Yeah?" he said, shoving a hand in his pocket and shifting his weight from one foot to another. He could never tell his mother about what he'd done.

He almost walked away from his family, but not because he didn't love them. His mother had sacrificed so much to keep her family together, to keep them on the farm, to make sure that they had a good childhood, to the very best of her ability.

He had to appreciate that.

"I need you to fix the souvenir shop up." She named a sum. "That's what the new owner told me she could afford to pay when she asked me to see if I could hire someone here in Strawberry Sands to fix it up so she could open the shop as soon as she can. I know that there was a plumbing leak, and the water had been shut off, and I'm pretty sure there were some holes in the drywall and possibly it needs a new roof."

"Holy smokes. That's a lot of work." He hoped that the amount of money that his mother quoted would be enough for those repairs. She was talking at least three weeks' worth of work. If not more. He appreciated the work, though. He'd been doing all kinds of odd jobs in order to earn money and get his ranch. He'd been training horses on the side, planning to sell them, since a well-trained horse would bring a lot of money, and he'd do whatever he could to earn enough to buy the ranch he dreamed of.

"I told her I knew the perfect person. I know you'll do a good job, and this person is going to try to make a living here in Strawberry Sands. You know we need people moving in and businesses opening up."

"I know." The more businesses that moved in, the better it was for everyone, because it attracted tourists. And their tourist dollars.

Those tourist dollars were necessary for the rest of his family and their businesses. He'd do what he could to help.

"I need to give you this." His mother pulled her hand out of her pocket and held up the key.

"I didn't say I would do it," he said, even as he reached out to take the key from her proffered hand.

"I know you will." His mother smiled, and he couldn't disagree. She was right. If she asked him, he would do it.

"Do you have a number for the new owner?"

"They were moving. They weren't sure whether they would continue to have the same number or not, and they gave me permission to coordinate everything. They're also dealing with a funeral."

He lifted his chin in acknowledgment, not asking any more questions. Sometimes a death in the family made a person have to make hard decisions and changes. He assumed that was what happened in this instance. Maybe a mother had lost her daughter and needed to move to a new area, opening a shop. He didn't know what the connection was and didn't want to stand around talking about it. He wanted to think about the horse he was buying.

The job was perfect. It would help him get started reestablishing the money that he just poured out of his account.

And if the person had enough money to pay to have their store fixed up, they might hire him to landscape around it as well. It wouldn't be much, just the area in front of the sidewalk, and perhaps a little bit along both sides, although there wasn't much room between the buildings. The souvenir shop was right beside the diner though, and lots of people would see his handiwork, which could lead to more jobs.

He chatted with his mom a bit before he said he would go down and look at the building, and give her a list of the things that he thought needed to be done.

To his surprise, she offered to go with him.

They turned, walking down the sidewalk. He listened to his mother speak but couldn't quit thinking about the future.

His horse and the foundation of the ranch that he wanted.

But there was something missing. There had always been something missing.

And now, going back to the souvenir shop where Dakota had spent a couple of summers as a young girl, and they had played on the beach together, riding horses and running wild, had crystallized the idea that maybe he had made a mistake all those years ago when he turned her down.

His rodeo career had been huge. He was a name that was recognized everywhere, but…it was all over. The fame was gone, and maybe he would have been better off getting married and coming back home when she'd asked.

If he had done that, he'd probably already own a ranch, Dakota would be beside him, and they'd be training horses together.

He smiled. Life never turned out the way a person thought it would. If he and Dakota had gotten together all those years ago, they probably would be divorced by now.

One dream was nice to think about, and one wasn't, so he shifted his thoughts and tried to focus on the job at hand. Putting Dakota behind him for good.

After all, the memories were bittersweet.

Chapter 3

Nine years ago...

Dakota looked at the little stick in her hand. It was supposed to be just the one line, but in the last five minutes, a second line had appeared, making a plus sign.

Her heart dropped.

She'd done something she'd never done before. Two things actually. She'd watched her best friend in all the world win his first rodeo world championship in bareback riding.

She'd been pretty much on top of the world for him even though she hadn't ended up placing at all. Her fault, not Goldie's. A concentration error, and that half a second had cost her everything.

After she'd taken care of Goldie, she'd gone out with her friend slash boyfriend, Ryan Landry.

She and Ryan had been on again, off again. He didn't want to get too serious because he had been chasing championship dreams of his own. And he didn't want a wife and kids holding him back. He'd been very clear about that. So, they hung out together, and she considered him one of her best friends. He had the same values and morals that she did, and they got along really well together. Plus, they had those childhood memories that bound them, fun memories of riding horses on the beach, lying on the warm sands, and swimming in the cool waters of Lake Michigan.

But during the championship rodeo, they'd hung out with people they met during the championship week, some they knew well, some not so well, and some they'd just met, and they'd all gone out together.

Dakota had tried alcohol not long after she turned twenty-one, decided she didn't like it and wasn't interested in developing a taste for it, even if her friends told her it was necessary, and hadn't drunk anything since.

She'd seen the stupid mistakes people had made after they had consumed alcohol. And she made enough stupid mistakes on her own. She was serious about winning a barrel racing championship, and alcohol wasn't a part of those plans.

The night of the world championships, she'd been celebrating along with everyone else, and her normally reserved personality had loosened up a lot after her first beer. So she'd drunk more.

She woke up beside Ryan.

She had very little memory of what they did, but considering that neither one of them were wearing clothes, and she was sore in places that didn't have anything to do with barrel racing, it hadn't been hard to figure out at least some of what she'd done.

She left before he woke up. Their relationship had been casual, and she hadn't wanted to face him because he'd probably not wanted to do what they'd done any more than she had. She went home to Iowa, and she assumed he'd gone home, too.

She hadn't talked to him since that night. But now, it seemed like they had something that they needed to discuss.

What was she going to say?

She put her hand over her stomach. She supposed she could give the baby up for adoption and never say anything to Ryan. She knew how he felt. He'd been very clear about not wanting a wife or children hanging around his neck. And he'd been so excited about winning, full of plans and dreams to make it two years in a row.

He was already making plans to practice and get better, talking about things he could do to prepare, physically and mentally as well.

She knew this was going to blow his plans up big time, and he wasn't going to be happy about it. Not that Ryan had a temper, because he didn't. He was one of the most easygoing people she knew, but he was driven. Single-minded in his determination to be a champion and now a two-time champion. Did she really want to hold him back from that?

But she didn't want to raise a baby on her own. She lost her parents young, and she had no support other than her gram.

She smiled. Her grandma would take her in. She could live with her.

But she wanted her child to have a father. She hadn't had her parents for long, but she couldn't imagine not having a father.

She sighed, turning toward the mirror, looking up from the little stick in her hands at her reflection.

Her mouth was open, her face pale, her eyes big in her face, her freckles stood out like flies in white cream.

Her red hair always made her complexion seem sallow, and those freckles didn't help her appearance. She'd never have beautiful, porcelain skin.

But she had a lot of experience under her belt.

She also had a baby under her belt.

She sighed. She was smart to stay away from alcohol. Why couldn't she have stuck to that? She would never have ended up like she had if she hadn't been inebriated.

Except, she'd always had a weakness for Ryan.

Her phone rang, and she dropped the stick in surprise.

Grabbing the phone, hoping that it was Ryan, although he had no reason to call, since he hadn't called for the last month, and what would she say to him anyway?

But that thought was barely formed before it disappeared, because the name that came up on her screen was Gregory.

She swallowed down disappointment. Gregory was handsome, charismatic, and he had won the saddle bronc championship.

Ryan had been annoyed, because Gregory was mostly a jerk.

Dakota had gone out with him a few times, but as handsome and charismatic as he was, he wasn't Ryan, and she liked

Ryan's calm sense of humor over Gregory's need to show off.

"Hello?"

"Hey, girl. How's the queen of the rodeo?" That's what he always called her, even though she knew she was no such thing and never would be.

"I'm fine."

What a lie. She didn't know she was capable of such a lie.

"I just want to know if you wanted to go out tonight. I feel like we didn't celebrate nearly enough, and I'm in town."

"Well, I actually was just leaving. I'm going to go see my grandma. Maybe stay with her during the off-season."

She had been living with her friend, Casey, helping her give horseback riding lessons and training future barrel racers.

But she couldn't do that if she was pregnant. Well, she could, but she couldn't do that with a baby.

Not unless she had someone to help her watch the baby.

But she'd been raised by her grandma. She didn't want her baby to be raised by someone other than her.

"I thought we'd go to the new steakhouse." He named the one that had just opened. "The queen of the rodeo deserves a nice steak once in a while, doesn't she?"

He was charming. And he was awfully nice too. And generous. They'd always got along well, and she forced a smile to her face, even though he couldn't see it. "Seems to me like the saddle bronc riding champion deserves a steak as well."

"That's my girl. I'll pick you up at seven."

"I have to make a phone call first. I'll let you know."

"Dakota," he said, drawing out her name, a little pleading, in a comical way that he did to make her smile.

It worked, kinda. Although there were still worry lines creasing her brow. She was pregnant. She. Was. Pregnant.

She wasn't quite sure that it had completely sunk in yet.

"Give me a few minutes. I'll let you know."

"What about tomorrow night? Just give me a yes."

"Yes." If she couldn't make it tomorrow night, she had time to cancel. But she had to talk to Ryan. Had to let him know what she found out. Had to...somehow tell him that he was going to be a father.

She couldn't be going out with Gregory if she and Ryan were going to get together.

But considering they hadn't talked to each other for a month...

She had to call him.

She got off the phone with Gregory, not even sure what all she said, but knowing that she had a hard phone call in front of her.

Taking the box and the little stick, she shoved it down the side of the garbage can so that it wasn't lying on top, just in case Casey nosed around, although she doubted she would. Casey had enough things going on, she didn't need to stick her nose into Dakota's business.

Regardless, she couldn't just let the stuff lie on top. She wasn't ready to tell the world yet. She had to figure out how she was going to deal with it first.

Thankfully Casey was already out with her early-morning clients.

Dakota got dressed quickly and decided that the best place for her to have this conversation was in the stall with her horse. She had plenty of time, since Casey was giving a lesson, and she'd have the privacy she needed. But being with Goldie always calmed her down, and this was a conversation that she was going to have to have a lot of courage in order to initiate.

Maybe the reason that Ryan hadn't called her at all was because he knew what they had done and...regretted it? Had there been some kind of problem with her?

She didn't remember much from the night. Nothing bad, anyway. She had no idea what Ryan's problem might be. None. And she liked him as a friend, and maybe wouldn't mind being more, obvi-ously since when she had enough alcohol in her system, she gravitated toward him, probably the way she wanted to but never allowed herself to.

Maybe she threw herself at him. Maybe he hadn't had a choice.

All kinds of terrible scenarios reared up in her head, and they weren't making the phone call she had to make any easier.

She tried to shove those thoughts aside and focus on all the positive things.

Maybe she'd wowed him with her prowess and he was too intimidated to try to call her again but was secretly hoping she would.

She laughed out loud. That was positive thinking, possibly, but more likely it was just comedic thinking, but it made her laugh.

Regardless, laughter eased some of the tension inside of her, and she mentally shrugged her shoulders. What was going to happen? He was going to tell her it was a terrible night and he didn't want to have anything to do with her? All right. She could handle that and move on with her life.

Except, the idea made her a little sad. Ryan wasn't that shallow, first of all. But second, she didn't want to think that they were incompatible. She knew she didn't think that way. And she couldn't think of a man that she would rather have as the father of her child.

The biggest problem was she was ashamed of her sin, which was the real reason she didn't want to make the call.

It took thirty minutes of brushing Goldie before she was calm enough to pull her phone out of her pocket and call the number she had memorized.

It rang so long she thought he wasn't going to answer. But then, his familiar voice came on the phone.

"Dakota?"

"Ryan." She sounded breathless. She hated that. She swallowed, took a breath, trying to sound calm. She couldn't lead off with, "I'm pregnant, and it's yours," so she tried to think of something else to say. "How are you?"

"Good. You?"

He didn't sound the slightest bit welcoming. How was she going to be able to tell him about the baby? Did she want to if he was going to be unfriendly and cold? She already knew he wasn't going to be happy about that. He obviously wasn't happy about what they'd done. He'd never been this off-putting to her before.

She had just taken a breath to tell Ryan straight out the reason that she was calling. I'm pregnant.

Two little words she needed to say, but she just couldn't seem to push them out, and then through the phone, she heard, "Ryan? Put the phone down and pay attention to me."

It was so close the woman's mouth had to be right next to the mouthpiece on his phone. Which meant she was standing close enough to Ryan to be touching him, holding him—Dakota glanced at the time—waking up with him.

Her stomach flipped and spun and curled and flinched, and she could hardly breathe.

"Sorry. I didn't realize you were busy." She somehow managed to push the words out, but she knew she sounded gutted. That was exactly how she felt. She couldn't pretend otherwise. She hadn't realized that she had such feelings for Ryan. She should have known, when she ended up in bed with him, that there was more to it, because alcohol or no, she wouldn't end up like that with just anyone. But the idea of him with someone else, waking up with someone else, holding someone else, she could hardly stand it.

"Yeah. I gotta go."

Was that regret in his tone? Disgust? She wasn't sure.

"Marry me, Ryan?" she said, hating the desperation in her voice, but at the same time, the words shocked her. She was supposed to be telling him she was pregnant, not asking him to marry her.

"You're not serious."

"Yes. I am. Please. Marry me?" She wanted a father for her baby, needed someone, didn't want to do this by herself.

She didn't know how to raise a child. She knew about horses, riding them, barrel racing, that was what she was good at. Kids? She knew nothing.

"You know I'm not ready to get married. I want to earn a back-to-back championship."

What could she say to that? She tried not to cry. She couldn't help it. But now she knew how he would react to her news—he wouldn't want to have anything to do with her or her baby.

And more than that, if she told him, and if he felt honor bound to marry her, he would forfeit the possibility of winning again and would lose the money he could earn from sponsors next year, and she'd basically be blowing up his entire life.

Unless she handled this herself and, in the process, set him free to be everything he was destined to be.

"Sorry." She didn't know what else to say.

"Yeah. I'll see you around."

"But—" Her voice broke off. He hadn't even entertained the idea of marrying her. Acted like she wasn't even serious.

How could she tell him she was having his baby?

Wasn't that the morally right thing to do? Except, when a woman knew that the man didn't want a child, when he'd been clear about that, when there had never been any question about whether or not he wanted to be a father, then it was okay for her to decide to allow him to go free, to take responsibility for everything and give him the space he needed to chase his dreams. After all, even if she just loved him as her friend, love was about putting the other person first.

And she would handle her baby by herself.

Maybe that wasn't fair, maybe that wasn't right, but it was her choice. She could give so that he could reach his dreams. It was a sacrifice that she could make.

She would consider the baby hers, not theirs, not his, and she would handle it. She would do that because Ryan deserved to not have that weight around his neck, he deserved to not have that kind of responsibility. He deserved a chance to win a second championship. He had the ability, and he could do it. But not if he was trying to support a wife and child.

She wouldn't ask him to be a father. But she did want to have a father for her baby.

"Yeah?" he prompted, and it felt like there was a little compassion in his voice.

"Ryan," the woman's voice said again, and she dragged his name out like she was running her finger down his arm at the same time she was saying it and blinking big, beautiful eyes up at him.

"Nothing. Take care."

She didn't hold the phone to her ear, waiting to see if he said anything in return, but took it down and swiped off.

That was that. The child was hers. She wasn't going to ask him to take on any responsibility.

She'd figure things out for herself.

Chapter 4

It hadn't been hard to figure it out. The next night, she went out with Gregory, and he'd pointed out that the press was calling him the king of the rodeo, and he'd always called her the queen. He said wouldn't it be fun if the king and queen ran off to Las Vegas and got married?

She hadn't really thought that would be fun, but it would solve the problem she had. She was pregnant with another man's child, needed a father for her baby. Didn't want to raise a child as a single mom and wanted her little one to have a dad.

So, she made the second biggest mistake of her life. Or was it the first? In the years to come, she'd go from thinking that sleeping with Ryan had been the biggest mistake she'd ever made to marrying Gregory was the biggest mistake. Maybe they were tied for first. It didn't matter, because she'd messed up her life.

She had that baby and then another, and then she and Gregory had gotten divorced.

And she ended up living with her gram anyway.

She barely made a living giving horse-back riding lessons, and in order to make ends meet, she ended up selling her horses one by one until Goldie was the only one left. By the time her grandma passed away, the only thing she had was the souvenir shop she'd inherited at Strawberry Sands and Goldie.

Goldie wasn't going to be able to make her a living; it would take time and money that she didn't have, and so she did the only thing that was possible for her to do.

Her gram died, she came home from the funeral, texted a friend who agreed to offer Goldie on several social media sites, taking that burden off of Dakota while she took care of her grandmother's things and mourned.

It wasn't long after that, money had been wired into her account, and she had enough to fix up the souvenir shop, purchase inventory, and move her children to Strawberry Sands.

It was the only thing she knew to do. Hopefully, she wouldn't have three things tied for the biggest mistake of her life.

Chapter 5

"Are we there yet?" Rachel asked, the whine in her tone as pronounced as it had been for the last three hours. "I have to pee."

"Well, guess what? This is the town, and pretty soon, we're going to see our new home," Dakota said, trying to sound enthusiastic.

She slipped into somewhat of a depression since she sold Goldie. It had taken longer than what she thought it would in order to get things straightened out with her sister, and then Rachel had a program she had been practicing for and she didn't want to miss. So Dakota had stayed a few extra days.

Although, she felt like every day counted. It was starting to get warm, and the tourist season would be in full swing in Strawberry Sands. Such as it was. She didn't really remember it ever being much to speak of, but if she wanted to make a living there, she was going to need to take advantage of every summer day.

"Here?" Maddie asked quietly, shifting in the back seat as she looked out the window. She had slept a good bit of the way. Maddie was her calm, easygoing child.

She took after her father.

Dakota hadn't allowed herself to think about things like that. Hadn't allowed herself to sit and reflect or to even re-member that her children had differ-ent dads. She didn't want to acciden-tally tell them sometime. Although, the idea that she needed to was there in her head. The girls deserved a dad. Al-though, Dakota seemed to excel at pick-ing men who didn't care about their kids.

That wasn't fair. Ryan hadn't had a chance. Although, if he had cared about them, it would only have been from a sense of duty. Since he had been very clear about not wanting children.

Normally she didn't sit around and think about those things. Water under the bridge was just that, water under the bridge that she couldn't get back. Nor did she want it. But she supposed commitment to Strawberry Sands dug up those old memories. Or maybe it was selling Goldie. Or possibly the combination of both. That and the fact that her life had blown up, and she lost the only person who had always helped her hold things together. The loss of her gram had hit her hard, and if she didn't have two children to take care of, she would probably still be in bed. With the covers pulled up over her head, crying because now she had to face life alone.

Except, she had to adult, because she had two children to raise. And there wasn't anyone to help her. No safety net to fall back on, and no one who really cared.

She still had friends from her rodeo days, but a lot of those people were just as broken as she was.

Chasing a dream was nice in theory, but in reality, it often left the person broke, broken, and regretful of their many bad choices.

The championship she almost won was nice to think back on, but she would trade that in a heartbeat for a steady family, a good husband, and a little bit of security by the way of a regular house payment, and friends and neighbors she could rely on.

Not friends and neighbors who were scattered across the country, and nothing to her name except a run-down souvenir shop that hadn't seen business for more than fifteen years.

Hopefully the money she sent to Mrs. Lana, her gram's friend, and the woman that her gram promised her would help her get her shop back up and running or at least fixed up enough that she could stay in it without getting wet when it rained, would be enough to get her started until she was making money on her own.

If this didn't work out, she had no idea what she was going to do.

Lord, I need You. I know in the past I've had a tendency to walk away from You when I thought I had everything under control. Although having everything under control is just an illusion. I know that now. I need You to help me. I have to provide for my children, I have to...survive. Somehow. Please.

She wished that she had been smarter, wiser, when she had been younger. She would have ditched the idea of being a rodeo queen and embraced the idea of having a solid home and all the things that she now wished she'd been working toward. A job. An education. An ability to support herself.

No point in looking back.

"Mom. I really have to pee."

She pulled herself from thoughts of the past and tried to focus on the present.

"All right. We're here. Just wait until I dig up the key, and we'll go to the bathroom right away." She hadn't wanted to stop a half an hour ago when Rachel first said she needed to use the restroom. They were almost there, and she hadn't wanted to make one more stop. Not that there had been any places to use other than just stopping along the side of the road.

Maybe part of her hoped that Ryan was in town. But most of her dreaded the idea of meeting him again.

He was probably married with a couple of kids of his own and living somewhere out west, not in Michigan. Hopefully. Since he was just one more thing she didn't want to have to face.

But part of being an adult was facing a whole pile of things that she didn't want to. She'd figured that much out, anyway.

"All right. You guys can hop out, and I'll dig out the key, and we'll go in and check out our new place."

"This is it?" Rachel asked, sounding like she hoped it wasn't.

"It is. You can even see the lake from here." She remembered that about her childhood. She had the spare bedroom on the second floor, and she'd spent more than one night watching the moonlight play on the water.

And most of her days running along the shores of Lake Michigan and riding horses with Ryan.

Funny how just a few weeks or months of her life could define it so perfectly.

She could only recall spending the majority of two summers in Strawberry Sands, but that defined so much of her childhood and made up a big portion of the memories that made her smile.

Holding the key in her hand, she walked toward the front door. She actually wasn't sure which door the key opened, but if she recalled correctly, the same key opened both the front door and the back door that went directly to the residence and the stairs that led up to the bedrooms.

There wasn't much living area behind and above the shop, but it would work for the girls and her. It was better than being homeless or living in a women's shelter.

She didn't even want to think that could be her next step.

A deep longing went through her. A longing for her horse and the rodeo circuit and all the dreams that had crashed and burned and lay in ashes at her feet.

Now she was facing things like women's shelters and bridges.

Even the small-town, cozy atmosphere of Strawberry Sands couldn't completely eradicate her fear of being homeless with her children. Or worse yet, having her girls taken from her.

"Do they have a school in this town?" Maddie asked, and the question made Dakota smile.

Maddie was quiet and responsible, easygoing, and she hardly ever got upset about anything.

Rachel was the exact opposite, emotional over everything, and everything was a major emergency, from needing to use the restroom to getting a paper cut.

"Mom, I have to pee," she said. This time, there was a lot of whine in her tone and more than a little bit of urgency.

"All right. I'm hurrying." She didn't have time to think about the memories, didn't have time to prepare herself or to worry about the future. Right now, she needed to find a restroom for her daughter, then she'd figure out how she was going to feed them.

Talk about taking care of the urgent and letting go of the necessary.

When she opened the door, she was in a bit of a rush, fearing that her daughter was going to pee herself just steps from the toilet. So, it was probably excusable for her to not recognize the man who was standing on a ladder, spreading spackling on a spot on the ceiling, his hand up, his eyes wide, and surprise in every feature.

His presence shocked her and brought her up short. Then, she remembered that she had asked Miss Lana to start repairs on the souvenir shop so she could get started with her business as soon as she arrived. She'd given some of the precious money she had made from selling Goldie to invest in repairs, trusting Miss Lana because her gram said she could.

Gram had said that Miss Lana was a good friend, but all Dakota remembered from those summers long ago was the horses and the beach...and Ryan.

"Excuse me. I'm the owner."

The man, stubble on his chin and a ball cap low over his eyes, stood at the top of the ladder, staring at her. When she introduced herself, it was punctuated by a crash, which Dakota realized was him dropping his spackling tool.

"Dakota?" He said her name tentatively.

Maybe that was what clued her in. Maybe it was the timbre of his voice. It had been years, and with the low ball cap and the stubble, she didn't recognize him right away. But that tone. It still sent shivers up her spine. Good shivers, and bad ones.

The very person she was hoping to not meet happened to be the first person she did.

"Ryan." She wanted to be calm, cool, and collected. To walk right by him without a second glance. To not let him know how his presence affected her. To shove the memories aside and focus on all the things that she needed to do, but she wasn't able to do that. "You're here."

"Yeah. I'm supposed to be. My mom said I was supposed to fix this up for the new owner… I guess that's you."

"Yeah. It's me."

"I peed my pants. Don't be mad, Mommy. I told you I had to go." Rachel started to cry.

Dakota's mouth was dry, she could hardly function, and those words seemed to come from a long ways away. "Sorry, sweetie. It's all my fault."

Of all the times she dreamed about meeting Ryan again, this was not one of the scenarios she had imagined.

"Excuse me," she said, feeling like she needed to say something to Ryan because he was still staring at her with his mouth open like he'd seen a ghost.

She felt like she had. Maybe he felt the same way.

Regardless, she couldn't stand around. She had a daughter with wet pants who was crying and thinking she was in big trouble. Or maybe embarrassed. Or a combination of both.

"I'll be right back. I'm going to grab your suitcase that has your clean clothes in it, then we'll go find a restroom."

"I wanted to go. You wouldn't stop. Now I'm all wet. It's your fault." Her daughter's voice raised with each sentence, until it became a wail and she started sobbing uncontrollably in the middle of the floor.

Exhausted from the trip, already frazzled because she didn't know what she was going to do, Dakota didn't know what else to do except go outside and get the suitcase. She wanted to stand in the middle of the floor and cry too.

But that had never solved anything. She'd done a lot of crying after she found out she was pregnant and even more after she married Gregory and realized what a mistake she'd made. Regret lived big and large, and the knowledge that she was going to be living a lie, unless she admitted to Gregory that she was carrying another man's baby.

In her youthful stupidity and inconsideration and foolishness, she had never done that, even though the information lay hot and heavy on her throughout their short marriage.

She couldn't blame Gregory entirely for the destruction of their marriage, although he had been the one who had cheated and left her.

Maybe he'd known deep down that she would never really care for him.

Grabbing the suitcase, she hurried back in, where her daughter still stood in the middle of the floor crying. She tried to grab her hand and pull her along, but Rachel dug her feet in and wouldn't budge. This was the kind of dramatics that Rachel was famous for. It was just Dakota's luck that she would choose right now to do it.

Ryan had come down off the ladder and picked up his spackling tool, but had been standing in the middle of the floor, seemingly indecisive as to whether or not he should go over and try to comfort the crying girl, and there was no doubt his look held relief as she walked in.

"I'm sorry to bother you. We'll try to stay in the living quarters." She had to yell to be heard over her daughter, and whatever Ryan said was lost in the angry screams of her little girl.

Finally, Dakota didn't know what else to do except put her arm around her daughter and pick her up. As soon as she did, Rachel wrapped her legs around Dakota's waist and pressed her wet body against Dakota, soaking them both.

Dakota had been hoping not to have to change her clothes, but that was pointless as well.

She needed the restroom, she needed more suitcases, she needed...a double dose of some kind of very strong pain medicine and a comfortable bed, but she had to make the bed first. If there even was one. She had to feed her girls, had to do a hundred things on a list a mile long.

Just once, just once in her life, she would really appreciate it if things would work out.

Anytime a thought like that came into her head, she thought about all the girls who dreamed of living the rodeo life she had, owning a horse of the caliber of Goldie, and being able to chase her dreams for years.

She wanted to tell those girls that those dreams were worthless. Sure, it was a nice five minutes of fame, and it was a nice thing to look back on, but it hadn't prepared her for anything else that she had to do in her life. And if she could go back, she would happily exchange the time she'd spent on the rodeo for something that truly mattered. Although, part of her wondered what that really was.

Chapter 6

Ryan couldn't believe it. Dakota was back in town. She was the one who was starting up a souvenir shop. It had been on the tip of his tongue to tell her that he had just bought Goldie, but he hardly thought that would be information she would welcome. Or maybe she already knew.

He hadn't expected seeing her again would evoke so many emotions in him.

But the last time he'd seen her...was the best and worst night of his life. Of course there would be emotion involved in that.

Nine years ago...

Ryan looked at the scoreboard, knowing Dakota hadn't even made it to the finals. There would be no barrel racing world championship for her this year.

He tried to fight back disappointment, because it would have been amazing if they'd both won a championship the same year.

Sure, they were competitors, but not against each other. He didn't want to think that's why they got along so well. He would root for her, even if she were competing against him, which she wasn't. But...he almost thought that she would do the same.

He wanted the championship, he wanted it so bad he could taste it, and she... She just seemed to be doing it for fun. Sure, she was serious about training and about practicing and about winning, but she didn't crave it the way he did.

Regardless, he found himself joining in the celebration and knew Dakota was truly happy for him. She glowed, more beautiful than he'd ever seen her. Of course, she was garnering attention from all of the guys in the group, some of whom he didn't even know. They were hanging out with people they didn't typically hang out with, and he found himself doing things he typically didn't, like ordering a beer, and then another, and dancing with his best friend.

She was soft and supple under his hands, muscular and slender, but with curves in all the right places. She smiled up at him with a glow in her eyes and something akin to hero worship. It made him feel like he could conquer the world.

When the music slowed, and her arms tightened around his neck and his around her waist and she laid her cheek against his and whispered in his ear that of all the men in the room, she thought he was the best, it did something to his already puffed-up pride, and it wasn't long after that that he suggested that they leave, and she eagerly nodded.

He led her down the sidewalk to the bedroom that he rented from the father of one of his friends who owned a riding stable and tack shop at the edge of town.

He'd been happy there for the couple months that he spent, and somehow having Dakota holding onto him and walking behind him made the place feel a little less cramped and more like a castle. Or maybe that was the alcohol.

Regardless, he woke up the next morning alone but very aware of what happened.

Aware and ashamed. He couldn't believe what he had done. His entire family would be disappointed in him, not to mention he couldn't look his best friend in the eye ever again. After all, that wasn't the kind of man he was. And maybe it had mostly been the alcohol, but he realized that for a while his feelings for Dakota had been deepening into something else. But she knew he didn't want a wife or family. Especially not now when the opportunity for a second championship was so close.

He would just allow her to lead the way on how they were going to handle it. She was the woman, and he'd follow her lead. That seemed like the best thing. And when she hadn't texted, hadn't called, hadn't contacted him at all, and his friend's dad who owned the riding stable offered him a position in the off-season teaching clients how to ride from beginner to advanced, he eagerly accepted, because he knew Dakota would be heading back to stay with her gram in Iowa.

He wanted the distance between them, except he missed her. Missed hanging out with her, missed talking to her, missed just having her smile greet him in the morning.

They spent so much time on the rodeo circuit together that she felt like a part of his life.

And it felt like there was a piece missing.

It took him a month, but he finally came to the conclusion that he needed to stop thinking about Dakota and realize that what happened between them probably ruined their friendship forever.

It was shortly after that that he got an early morning phone call from her, just as he was giving Gina, the daughter of his boss, her first riding lesson.

Gina had been angling for them to be more than instructor and student, and when he informed her that he planned to focus completely on winning a championship and didn't want to be encumbered with a girlfriend, she insisted to her dad that she wanted him, and only him, to give her riding lessons.

She had been standing at his elbow when he answered Dakota's phone call. Seeing Dakota's number pop up on his phone had sent all kinds of crazy reactions going through his body, but he didn't want Gina to see how he responded to the call.

He hadn't known what to say to Dakota, hadn't wanted to talk to her in front of Gina, and hadn't responded well at all.

Before he was able to call her back when he had time and privacy, he'd heard from a friend who'd seen on the news that she had eloped and married Gregory, and the press was calling them the king and queen of the rodeo, and that had struck daggers into Ryan's heart.

The woman he considered one of his best friends, if not his very best friend, had gone and married the man who had won the title of saddle bronc champion.

He didn't think he'd ever get over it.

Fast forward nine years, and here she was, in the same building as him, two of her children with her, and him unable to leave because he promised his mother he would fix up the building for the new owner, which he had not known was Dakota.

Had his mother known? But his mother didn't know his history with Dakota. All she knew was that he and Dakota had been friends when they'd been children when they'd been around eight or nine years old. Something like that. He'd never told his family that he met her again on the rodeo circuit, although they might have guessed, considering that the folks who followed the circuit were usually good friends. And if not good friends, they at least knew each other.

He had almost finished up for the day, and he decided to quit early. He probably should offer to help Dakota carry her things in from the car, but all she had was her car; there was no U-Haul, no trailer, nothing to show that she brought anything other than what would fit in what she drove.

Maybe her furniture and that type of thing was coming the next day. He'd been upstairs with his mom whenever they had looked at what all needed to be fixed. There was nothing upstairs, not a bed, not a table, just an old stove and refrigerator, which he wasn't even sure still worked.

He could see occasional movement out front as Dakota went to her car, but she did not walk through the storefront again, carrying her things around the back.

It made him sad. Part of him wished that they could go back to just being friends. The easy camaraderie, the fun laughter, and the way she always got him. Or even when she didn't get him, she provided a balance for him. No one was perfect, but Dakota had always felt perfect for him.

That night had ruined everything. He felt guilty. He had no idea what she felt, and he allowed that to come between them. Allowed his guilt and shame that he felt for what he had done to ruin one of the best friendships he ever had.

He should apologize.

He cleaned his things up, setting everything aside, and took one last look around, making a mental note of the things that he still needed to do. There was a lot, and he didn't know where Dakota would want him to focus. But he needed to take a walk to clear his head, and he did the only thing that he knew would help. He went to the stables, got a brush, and started grooming Goldie.

Goldie seemed like the link between Dakota and himself.

Lord, I'm so sorry for what I did. I know You've forgiven me, but is there any way to bridge the gap between Dakota and me?

He wanted his friend back. Maybe he wanted more, although he only heard rumors that she and Gregory had separated. He didn't know for sure they were even true. She could still be married. Or married to someone else.

When his phone rang, he couldn't believe the relief that surged through him when he saw that it was his mother. She would know the answers to his questions. Although asking those questions would make her suspicious.

"Hello," he said, putting his phone on speaker and setting it on the hayrack so he could continue to brush Goldie. Her coat shone with health, and he was grateful once again to whoever had her before he had. The horse was in excellent health and had been well taken care of. Whoever had owned her had done a great job.

"Ryan. I just wanted to let you know that Dakota arrived in town. I drove by on my way to the diner and saw your pickup wasn't there anymore. I thought you might want to give her a hand moving in."

"I was there when she got there. Did a trailer or something arrive with her things?"

"No. As far as I know, she just has the car."

"Didn't seem to me like she could fit much in there."

"You saw her?"

"Yeah. Not for long," he added quickly.

"And you didn't help her?"

"There wasn't much for her to do," he said, but his mother's question made him feel guilty. He should have helped. He just...had some things he needed to wade through first, and her children were between them.

"Oh," his mom said, and he could hear the disappointment in her voice. She didn't have to say anything to him.

"Things are kind of complicated between Dakota and me."

"Oh." This one had a different tone. It invited him to explain what the complications were.

He needed some wisdom in his life. His mom was the wisest person he knew. But in order for her to be able to give him good advice, he was going to have to admit what he had done. He wasn't looking forward to that. He would rather just push that all under the rug and not have anyone know.

"You know Dakota and I used to be pretty good friends."

"I know when she was here visiting her gram during the summers when you guys were little, you were inseparable.

You both loved horses, and whenever she was here, I could count on you wanting to be with her, whatever it was you guys would be doing."

He smiled at the memories. "Yeah." But then he realized his mom didn't know. "We were good friends while I was on the rodeo circuit too."

"You didn't tell me much about those years. You were gone a good bit, and when you were home, you had some good stories, but typically they were not stories that gave too much insight into your personal life."

"I really didn't have much of a personal life during that time. I was focused on winning a championship. I pretty much put everything I had into it."

"You and Dakota were friends?" his mother prodded gently.

His hands stopped on Goldie's shining coat. She already glistened, but the rhythm of brushing her was soothing, and he forced his hands to move again.

"Yeah. We were friends. Good friends. I considered her my best friend for a long time."

"I didn't know."

"Yeah." They had the memories together from their childhood, but they also had so much in common. While they didn't think alike, they complemented each other in that way. They had different interests, and that enabled their friendship to deepen, and they never allowed the things that they didn't agree on to come between them. She just...suited him so perfectly. He had been a fool not to see that before.

"She was a pretty awesome person. Always willing to lend a hand, and always wanting to help me if she could."

"That's rare."

"Yeah. Dakota is a very rare kind of person." He could see that now too.

"What happened?" his mom asked, again bringing him back to the present.

"Well..." He took a breath, trying to figure out how he was going to say this. He didn't have to tell his mom. She didn't need to know everything about his private life, and more than likely, she didn't want to. But she couldn't tell him how to proceed, if he didn't tell her what he'd done, and... He kinda thought it would be good to confess. "When I won my first rodeo championship, before she got married, she and I spent the night together."

His mom gasped.

"We had both been drinking. I didn't drink as a general rule, ever. Neither did she. But that night... I guess we both were hanging out with people we usually didn't, and we did a lot of things we usually didn't. I regret it. I suppose she probably does too."

"You didn't ask her? You guys didn't talk about it?"

"I haven't talked to her since that night. Well, just once. On the phone when she randomly called me."

"What did she want?"

"Well... I wasn't really able to talk at the time. I was in the middle of giving a lesson." He winced, remembering how brusque he'd been on the phone, all because he'd had Gina at his elbow and hadn't wanted to speak with Dakota right then. He'd wanted privacy for their conversation, planned to call her back later.

As if reading his mind, his mother asked, "And you never called her back?"

"No. And then she got married. Just a couple of days later. Maybe she was going to tell me that." Although, from all the news reports, they had decided just that night before. It wasn't a premeditated thing. I read the news reports about her getting married. If she knew about it before they did it, they did a good job of pretending she didn't."

His mother sighed. "I guess you can't always believe everything you read online."

"No. You can't." She didn't call to tell him she was getting married. He was almost sure of it. Maybe she was calling to apologize. Maybe she was going to try to get their friendship back. He wasn't sure. He supposed it was long enough ago that it didn't matter.

"She's divorced now. Her grandmother just died. And she had to sell everything, even her horse. She is about as low as a person can go. I was hoping you would be friends with her."

"She sold her horse?" Of all the things his mother had said, that was the one that struck him the most.

"Yeah. She was one that she almost won the barrel racing championship on or something. She was worth a lot of money. But she had to make a choice as to whether she was going to feed her children, or whether she was going to keep the horse. I think she chose the correct thing."

"Yeah. She did."

And he had Goldie. Boy, he could hardly imagine what Dakota would say when she found out. Would she be upset?

Would she be relieved? Would she hate him even more than she already did?

He assumed she hated him. Why else would she have married Gregory? As far as he knew, she had the same feelings toward Gregory that he did. The guy was a good rider, but he was arrogant and annoying.

"I just know she's had a hard life. She doesn't have anyone in the world, other than her sister whom she's not very close to. I was hoping that here in Strawberry Sands we could make her part of our family."

"No. Mom. Did you not hear me? I ruined our friendship by spending the night with her. We...can't do the friend thing anymore."

That was icky. He didn't want to talk to his mom about that. He pinched the bridge of his nose. This was not a conversation he wanted to go any further.

"Listen, when you sin, you have guilt. It leaves scars, and it makes you regret things. But you can't expect the rest of the world to operate off of whatever it is that makes you uncomfortable. You need to face your sin, get forgiveness for it, and move on with your life."

He didn't want to listen to his mom, didn't want to hear that, even though he knew she was right. The whole reason that he wanted to talk to her was because he knew that she would have wisdom for his situation. And it was right there; that was what he needed to do. He needed to apologize to Dakota and get forgiveness. Otherwise, if his mom insisted that they needed to include Dakota in family functions, everything was going to be extremely awkward.

"I know you're right, Mom. I don't really want to hear it, but I suppose the right thing is not usually the easy thing." He ran a hand down Goldie's back. Her fur was soft against his palm, smooth like satin. This was the horse that Dakota loved, and somehow he had ended up with her. He ended up in Dakota's building, fixing her shop. His mom had gotten involved, and it seemed like everywhere he turned in his life, Dakota was there.

Lord? I suppose this means I'm supposed to be doing something, but You know I can be kind of dense. What is it that I'm supposed to be doing?

Apologizing for one. Helping her for another? Even though he didn't want to. He wanted to stay far away from her, except he wanted to be close too.

"So I apologize. I ask for her forgiveness, and then what?" he said, knowing his mom always had thoughts about things. Usually, she was right.

"I understand you have history, but she's here, and if you are going to be a friend at all, she needs you now. She needs someone, anyone. Maybe you can be a blessing to her. Once you find out what you can do, put the effort into being a blessing."

That sounded simple, and maybe it would be, once he got past the apologizing.

"Thanks, Mom. I can always depend on you to give me straight talk, even if it isn't what I want to hear."

"And I can always count on you to do the right thing,"

"No. I'm pretty sure I just told you I didn't do the right thing."

"That was years ago, Ryan. I'm going to assume that it isn't going to happen again."

He hadn't touched alcohol since. And while he dated a few times, he'd never done anything even remotely close to what he'd done with Dakota. For some reason, while his body was willing, his mind was not. Seemed like his brain was stuck on her.

Even though she hadn't been stuck on him. After all, she'd asked him to marry her and then turned around and married Gregory instead. Which was so unlike her that he'd been shocked by the news.

His eyes narrowed. Why would she have done that?

Chapter 7

Dakota managed to avoid Ryan the entire next day as she and her girls settled into their apartment. She had to make a trip to buy a couple mattresses and a couple small pieces of used furniture, and for the time being, until she saw how her money held out, they were going to make do.

In the meantime, the girls and her were subsiding on dry cereal, crackers, and cookies. Her girls didn't mind that at all.

She allowed them one day to get settled in, and then the next day, she took them to the school to register them and get them started.

It took longer than she was expecting, and she was starving by the time she got back to Strawberry Sands.

She had a ton of things to do, and she was grateful that the school would feed the girls at least. They'd have one healthy meal that day.

As for her, she was pretty sure they ate all the cookies and crackers, and it looked like it was going to be dry cereal for lunch.

Smells from the diner wafted toward her, but she tried to ignore them as she closed her car door and walked around the car.

She stopped abruptly as Ryan walked out the front door of the shop and stood in front of her on the sidewalk.

"Hi," she said, trying to sound dismissive and busy, ducking to go around him.

"I was hoping I could talk to you."

She had made it around him and started to take one more step when his words made her stop.

She didn't want to talk to him. Didn't want to look at him, didn't want to have anything to do with him. But she knew that that was probably wishful thinking. She needed to get over the feelings she had and try to be civil.

Although, that shouldn't involve a long, drawn-out conversation.

"Are you hungry?" His words were low, studiously so, if she had to take a guess based on their years of friendship.

She wanted to say not really. That was a lie. Even if it was the kind of lie that she didn't really think about as a lie, but more as a I don't want you to feel like you have to eat with me kind of answer, she couldn't force the words out.

Instead she told the truth. "I am."

"Let's grab something from the diner, and then head to the stable to eat. Or we could eat on the beach."

He knew she loved horses. Her heart had always been with the horses. She did barrel racing, but it wasn't because she loved the rodeo or loved the crowns or loved performing. It was because she loved horses.

"I think I'd rather not," she found herself saying.

"Please? I need to talk to you."

"Talk." She lifted her chin, turning around to look at him. "I have things to do."

"Let me help you with what you have to do, and we can talk while we're doing it."

"Let's get something to eat and go to the beach," she said immediately. If she had to spend time with him, she'd rather do it outside of her place. If he was in her space, she couldn't leave, but if she was at the beach, she could walk away when she was ready to and not have to spend any more time with him than what she had to. And while she loved horses, it wasn't something she wanted to share with him. So the beach it was.

"Thank you," Ryan said, and he sounded humble. It made her feel better immediately.

But being with him stirred the same old feelings. The ones that she'd ignored while she considered them just friends but had come roaring to life the night of the rodeo championship. That had led to the worst mistake, no, the second worst mistake she'd ever made.

"I can run to the diner and grab whatever it is that they have on special, if... Do you have anything you need to carry in and get ready to go?"

She jerked her head. "I can do it."

"Okay, fifteen minutes tops," he said, and then he touched her arm. She had to work to keep from yanking it away. "Thank you."

She didn't look up, just stared at where his hand touched her arm, the long brown fingers, blunt nails, and his gentle touch.

That touch stirred memories, gray and fuzzy, but still, it was more the feelings that she had to hide that bothered her.

She didn't want to spend any more time with him than what she had to. She could eat, let him say whatever it was he wanted to say, and then cut out as fast as she could.

With that thought in mind, she was back down waiting for him thirteen minutes later. He walked around the corner, carrying a brown paper bag in one hand and a plastic bag with what looked like drinks in another.

"I grabbed us two bottles of water. I didn't know if you still love Mountain Dew or not."

"I try not to drink it anymore." She shrugged her shoulder, not wanting to say that since she had children, she'd found it harder to stay slim than it had been before.

That was information he really didn't need to know. Things that she might have told him at one time, and they might have laughed about, but not anymore. She wasn't going to let her guard down. Ryan had ditched her when she needed him, and she wouldn't forget that.

He got her to go with him, but she didn't seem happy about it.

Ryan carried the food and drinks while Dakota walked beside him, her hands in her pockets, her eyes on the sidewalk.

He lifted his eyes toward the lake, then looked out over the pasture field where the horses grazed.

He had Goldie and the three geldings he was training on the far end of Matt's property, and it was at least a ten-minute walk around the pasture and a little more if they went by way of the beach, which is how he intended to go.

He should take the time to start talking to her, but he couldn't think of anything to say. He wanted to lead up to the apology but couldn't figure out what he wanted to say, only that he really wanted to get it out of the way.

"Would you like to sit here and eat?" he asked, indicating a small rise in front of the stable. He didn't think that she knew that he had bought her horse. He didn't even know if she owned her when he bought her. Almost certainly she didn't know that he had Goldie in his possession now since they'd both had other people handle the sale for them. Unusual, sure, but not unheard of. He could ask if she knew. But he wanted to apologize before they got distracted by her horse.

"That's fine," she said, sounding disinterested and like she truly didn't care where they ate or even if they did, although he heard her stomach growl twice on their walk, loud enough to be heard over the breeze that blew almost constantly from the lake.

"All right," he said, and then as they stopped, he said, "I'm sorry. I never thought to bring a blanket."

"It's okay. I don't need one."

"We ate on the beach all the time when we were kids, and a blanket was the last thing we ever thought of."

A little smile tilted up the corners of her mouth, but she still looked more like she was headed toward the Inquisition than having lunch with an old friend.

He waited for her to sit down, then sat beside her, but not too close, getting her food out, and then his, and giving them each a bottle of water. He prayed for the food and waited for her to open it.

"Griff is making strawberry rhubarb biscuits today. He has a cream cheese spread they're serving along with it, and I got some of that too. He wasn't a part of Strawberry Sands when we were growing up, but he's known for coming up with some really great combinations."

"Sounds good," she said, digging into her food like she was either starving or determined to get through it so she could leave.

The biscuits smelled good, along with the chicken salad and honey dressing Griff had to go with them. But he let his food lie in his lap.

"I wanted to apologize." There. He didn't have the fancy words to lead up to it, but he needed to say it, and so he would.

She pushed her hair back away from her face, then finished buttering the biscuit.

"You don't need to apologize," she said, and there was disinterest in her voice.

"I do. I... I wanted to. I needed to. I... I feel guilty for what I did."

"Well, don't. Those things happen. Lots of people do what we did. Obviously." She rolled her eyes.

"I don't do what we did. And it wasn't right for you."

"Fine. But you don't need to apologize for it."

"I ruined our friendship."

"I was there too. It wasn't just you." She sounded a little angry.

"I know. I wasn't trying to minimize your role. I was trying to take responsibility."

"You don't have to. The responsibility is on both of our shoulders. We were consenting adults, and we had sex. That happens."

She tossed her hair over her shoulder and put the biscuit in her mouth, chewing like she was being forced to and not like she enjoyed it.

He looked down at the food in his lap. She'd reduced what they did to what it was, but... It had been a little more than that to him.

"We didn't used to be like this. We used to...like each other." He gritted his teeth. "That night changed what we had, and I wanted to apologize for that."

"It wasn't that night that changed things," she said, after she swallowed. She picked up her fork and dug into her food.

"It was. It did."

She held a forkful in midair and looked at him, her eyes narrowed. "No. It wasn't."

"Things have changed, though. Am I right?"

"It was the phone call. That's what changed everything." She shoved food in her mouth and turned her face toward the lake, refusing to look at him.

The phone call. That changed everything?

For him, everything changed the night they'd spent together, and...maybe he'd fallen in love with her. Maybe he had already been. But she left, and he'd known that was what needed to happen. Because he wanted a championship. But if she had woken up in his arms, if she had admitted to enjoying the night as much as he had, could they have made things work? Would he have given up everything for her?

In hindsight, maybe life made him wiser. Maybe he was closer to the Lord now than he was then. Maybe experience had taught him that the championship was a worthless thing. Awards, accolades, whatever they were, they didn't matter. It was how a person treated other people. How they built their life based on biblical values, who they helped, who they served. How they lived for Jesus, not what they won or the money they made. Or even what kind of horse they bought.

"Do I owe you an apology for the phone call too?" She had asked him to marry her, out of the blue. How was he supposed to act at the time? "Why did you ask me to marry you?"

"I'm trying to figure out if you're really as clueless as you seem."

"I am. In my mind, everything was all about that night. It's what changed everything for me. I... It was the best night of my life. But you left. And I was afraid if I allowed everything to change, I would lose everything I had built."

She narrowed her eyes and looked at him. Except she wasn't looking at him. She wasn't talking to him. And she looked shocked and angry and cold. "Are you out of your mind? We were both drunk."

"I wasn't so drunk that I don't remember everything." He wanted to set his food aside, but instead his thumb traced the edge of the Styrofoam container. "I was with my best friend, and I felt like I...loved her." He lifted his eyes, unable to keep whatever emotion he was feeling inside from coming out on his features. He didn't even know how to school his face so that it wouldn't show...pain? He was feeling that. But also regret, deep regret.

He pushed the memories of that night aside. He'd tried to convince himself that he didn't feel anything for her, but it wasn't true.

She snorted and looked away. "I was so drunk I don't remember much of anything. I woke up, sick, with a hangover the size of Texas, and I looked over and you were naked in my bed. Or, rather, I was naked in yours. Not exactly something a girl is proud of. No one raised like I was anyway. I couldn't wait to get out of there. I was embarrassed and appalled. That wasn't what I was raised to be."

"Me either. But you can admit there was sin while still knowing that what you did was special."

She shrugged her shoulders. "I don't remember hardly anything. I told you that."

Was it true? Could she really not remember anything?

"Why did you call me?" Suddenly that was the burning question. Because she said the phone call was the problem.

She stood and put her hands on her hips. Ryan set his food aside as well and rose also, hoping she wasn't going to leave without answering. Without talking this through.

He didn't necessarily want to talk, but if they were going to be in the same small town, they had to figure something out. Or he supposed they could just brush it under the rug, but his mother would never be happy with that solution.

"I called you...because I was pregnant with your child." She kept her hands on her hips and faced him, like she was facing a firing squad. Like she expected him to attack her. Or in defiance, like she didn't care what he said, she was going to battle with him.

"Pregnant?" That was not what he was expecting. He hadn't even considered that. Although he should have. He had considered more the emotional implications of that night, which was really crazy, considering that he was a guy and he shouldn't care, except he did. He cared a lot. He wanted her to care too. Maybe she did. He thought back, then answered his own question.

"That's why you asked me to marry you." He was just putting it all together.

"Yeah. You pretty much shut that idea down."

"Why didn't you tell me you were pregnant?"

"How many times did you tell me you didn't want the burden of a wife or child or children? How many times had you said that you couldn't win a championship with that kind of ball and chain around your neck?"

She was right. He said that all the time back then. Being a father, being a husband, was about the worst thing he could think of. It would end everything, except... It would've been a good thing. To have a woman like Dakota beside him, to raise their children together, to... His mind stopped. Was one of the children that she had with her yesterday his?

That idea took his breath away.

He wanted to go directly to that, but that wasn't what she needed to talk about. And for once, maybe he had gotten wiser through the years, but he knew that what he felt wasn't the most important thing right now. He had let her down when she needed him. Even though she hadn't told him, he should've known that his best friend wasn't just going to call him up and ask him to marry her. But through the years, he'd been stuck on the night they had. And she didn't even remember it. Or didn't want to.

"So you knew that I didn't want children, but you asked me to marry you?"

She looked away.

"Dakota," he prompted her. Wanting her to explain. To tell him what he needed to hear. To make him understand what exactly was going on.

"I found out just a few minutes before I called you that I was pregnant. I hadn't even had time to process it myself. I just knew I didn't want to raise a child alone. I was scared, I... I wanted you. Not just as the father of my child, but as my friend."

"And I let you down."

"I didn't present it very well. I know I didn't. But I was so messed up. I regretted that night. I have some feelings from that night, but I really don't remember much of anything. And that wasn't the biggest thing. The biggest thing was that I knew that what we did was something that I probably had wanted to do for a long time and I just didn't realize it. But the baby changed everything. And when you said no to marrying me, I knew that that was what you were going to say anyway. And I had a choice. I could either tell you about the baby and crush all of your dreams, or I could suck it up and handle it myself."

"You put me ahead of you." He should have known. That was the way Dakota always was. She thought ahead and made decisions based on what was right. She had been wise. He had been the foolish one. Although, if he had known that she was pregnant with his child, he... What would he have done? Would he have given up the other championships?

He didn't have to make the decision. Dakota had taken it off his shoulders. She had made the decision for him.

"You made the sacrifice so that I could win championships."

"Yeah. Look at you. You wouldn't have three championships if I had made a different decision that day."

Chapter 9

Dakota looked down, but her hands continued to be perched on her hips, her stance combative.

"Any other questions?" she asked Ryan, lifting her chin and sounding disinterested. Like she didn't have any emotions involved, when he knew that was not true.

"You had two girls with you yesterday. Is one of those mine?"

"Maddie, the eight-year-old." One side of her mouth pulled back like she didn't really want to divulge that.

"I have a daughter. Maddie."

He couldn't help but smile. She had named her after one of their favorite horses. He met her eyes, and he could see that she realized he knew. She looked away before he saw her smile.

"I can't be mad at you for not telling me."

"No."

"Did Gregory know?" He didn't know where that question came from, but it seemed like a good one.

"No. There were a lot of secrets in our marriage, and that was one of them.

Some of the others were the girlfriends he had, ones I didn't know about."

"Gregory's a jerk," he muttered.

"Yeah."

"Is he paying child support?"

"No. I was afraid he would demand a paternity test, and obviously one of my daughters would have found out something they don't know. I... I know he was my husband and it was wrong of me to marry him without him knowing who the father of my child was, but I couldn't let that out, because you—"

"I wouldn't have the championships if you had said anything. I get it."

Stupid. The championships didn't mean anything. What were accomplishments versus a daughter?

"Well, when I asked for you to talk with me, this is not how I pictured this turning out."

"I found that most of the time, things don't quite turn out the way I picture them turning out," she said, and there was a little bit of irony in her voice, although she still didn't seem very friendly toward him.

"The way I wanted this to turn out was that you and I left friends. It still feels like…like you're mad at me. Maybe rightly so, but all I can do is apologize. And… Ask if I can have another chance."

"Another chance for what?" she said, her eyes narrowing with suspicion.

"I'm not asking for another night with you." Not really. Although, it had been a good night. And he supposed that maybe that was something he had in his head as a possibility. Marriage. Not a night of illicit sex. But marriage. Love. Rings. A family. A woman with character and convictions beside him, one who would sacrifice so much just to see him succeed, see him reach his dreams, see him do what he had always wanted to do, while she gave up everything.

Except for their daughter. She had her. And maybe Dakota knew all along that she had the most important thing.

But he had refused what she had offered him, which was herself. He had tossed her out of the way, the idea of marriage to her, and although he couldn't remember now how he had done it, he guessed that she had felt unwanted, unloved, and unworthy.

How could he convince her that that wasn't the case?

Not right away and definitely not now.

He swallowed, having no idea where to start. His goal for the conversation had been to be friends, but he hadn't realized there was so much between them.

"If we pass each other in the street, will you talk to me?" He supposed he should start there.

"Of course. Do you think I would ignore you?" she asked, sounding a little sarcastic.

"I guess you could. I suppose I kind of deserve it."

"You don't. All you did was refuse to marry me. It wasn't like you kicked me when I was down and you knew it."

"But it was a crazy request. I should have suspected there was something behind it to make you ask. I was giving a lesson when I was talking to you."

"I understand exactly what kind of lesson you were giving," she said, derision in her tone.

"It was the boss's daughter, Gina. You probably remember her."

She froze, then her lips curved up just a little. "I remember you complaining about her."

"Yeah. Well, I was completely booked during the day, and her dad insisted that I had to give her lessons. So it was early morning or nothing. And to my surprise, she actually got out of bed. For three lessons anyway."

"I see." Maybe she had thawed a little. He supposed it was a natural conclusion for her to think that there had been a woman with him, in bed. At that time, maybe he'd realized that, and maybe he'd wanted her to think that on some level. Although, he hated to think that he was that shallow.

"All right. So you would acknowledge me if we pass on the street. Am… Am I allowed to continue working on your shop?"

"I don't think there's anyone else. You already have the money. At least, I gave it to your mom."

"Did you know she was my mom?"

"No. All I had was her first name. I didn't ask questions. I was dealing with my grandma dying and my sister taking over the house and moving out and my daughters changing schools, and I just wanted to get started on the shop."

"I see." Then she probably didn't know that he bought her horse too. "Do you want to finish your food?"

"I wouldn't think I would say this, but I'm not hungry."

"I'm not really either. We can keep it. We'll be hungry later."

"Maybe."

"You're going to get hungry at some point."

"It doesn't feel like I'll ever be hungry again, but I suppose you might be right."

She dropped her hands and turned back toward the lake. She seemed to forget he was there, and he watched as the wind lifted her hair, similar to the graceful life of the manes and tails of the horses she loved. She'd always been so driven and determined, and yet she never allowed her ambition to get in the way of her treating people right. And despite her ambition, her drive, her desire to do everything right, she'd been willing to sacrifice in order for him to achieve his dreams.

He had never had anyone make a sacrifice of that magnitude for him. And she'd never told him, never expected him to do anything for her in return, never even breathed a word of it. If her grandma hadn't died, if she hadn't decided to open the souvenir shop, if his mother hadn't paved the way for her to be able to do that, Ryan might never have found out. Found out about Dakota's sacrifice, and the fact that he had a daughter.

A daughter.

He wanted to know her, wanted to meet her, but she didn't even know that he existed, let alone that he was her father. And he wasn't sure how to approach Dakota about that. He didn't want her to think that he only wanted to be around her because of their child. But he wanted her to know that he wanted to be in his daughter's life.

Realizing that she might take everything all wrong, he decided that he needed to say something anyway.

"I understand that our daughter doesn't know about me. Can we change that? I'd really like to get to know her. To...support her." He wasn't sure about that last part. He didn't want to drive a wedge between the sisters with one who had a dad who cared about her and one who didn't. "Actually, if you allow it, I'd like to get to know both of your daughters."

She wasn't looking at him, and he closed his eyes. He had never been interested in children at all. Not even a little. Something had definitely shifted within him in the last hour. Something huge, something that had an awful lot to do with the fact that Dakota had been so selfless.

"Yeah."

Her word was soft, almost carried away by the wind. She closed her eyes for a moment, as though drawing strength from something, and then she turned to him.

"I hope it's okay if we don't do it right away? I know, I would be angry right now if I were you. Furious that you had kept the fact that I had a child away from me. And I appreciate you not holding that against me."

He opened his mouth, opened it to tell her that he understood why she had done it. That she thought it was what he wanted, that she had done it at great sacrifice to herself, but also at a sacrifice to their child. Unintentional, but still a sacrifice, since the father that she had had not been kind or concerned.

"I would just like for her to be able to adjust to the move first. It's been a lot of changes in our lives. I swore after my grandma mostly raised me that I wouldn't dump my children off on any-one else to raise. That I would do it my-self if I could. Of course, I've had to have a job, but beyond that, I was there for them. But my grandma was still a huge part of their lives. They lost her, they lost the house that we were living in, I... She's just lost a lot."

He wondered if she was going to men-tion Goldie and wondered if he'd say anything, but she didn't. He wanted to ask about her, but it seemed like they already had so much between them, he didn't want to complicate things with the horse. He hadn't realized that their conversation was going to go in this di-rection. He wanted her to know about Goldie, but they had a lot of other things to wade through first. The horse could wait.

"But I can still come and keep fixing up the shop?" he asked again, feeling humble. He had the championships behind him, money from endorsements, and the ability to buy her horse, because of the sacrifice that she had made. It seemed like he shouldn't be asking for more.

"Yeah. I was hoping you would."

"I might see the girls."

"That's fine. It's not that I don't want you to see them. Please. I mean, you can start building a relationship without her realizing who you are, can't you?" Her face scrunched up, and she looked worried. "I'm not trying to keep her from you or anything." She bit her lip.

"No. I didn't think that. I... I get it. As an adult, I can only handle so much change, and as a child, I can't even imagine what she's gone through. Both of your girls." He added that, because he didn't want to just pick one of her girls and favor them, even if that one was his biological child.

He couldn't imagine someone coming in and picking one or two of his siblings and showering love on them but not him. It would feel so...divisive. Unfair. Hurtful.

"I don't want to make your other daughter feel unwelcome or unloved."

"Thank you. I do appreciate that. But I don't expect you to treat both of my children like they're yours. I...have to figure out how to tell them, and then they'll just have to accept the fact that one of them has a dad who wants to be involved in her life."

"I'm telling you, I want to be involved with both of them. I couldn't imagine someone coming into my family and only picking one or two of us to give attention to. I wouldn't want that done to me, how could I do that to your girls?"

She blinked, and then her eyes met his and they were wide. Like she couldn't understand why someone would talk like that. But he couldn't understand how someone wouldn't.

Of course, he'd never been faced with the situation before, and he hadn't known how he would react. He hadn't even really talked to the girls. Maybe that would change things, but he doubted it. He already loved his daughter, and he didn't know anything about her, other than she was his. How could he not love her sister the same way?

"I don't think I've ever heard anything like that before," she finally said softly, a little bit of wonder in her voice.

"Yeah. Well, don't give me too much credit. I'm sure there's lots of places where I'm going to screw up. I might even screw this up. But I'm going to try hard not to."

She snorted. "Isn't that what life is? We screw up, and then we just have to try to do better. But there's no such thing as a perfect life. Whatever we do, we're going to mess it up."

"We can accept it but not allow it to make us less vigilant about doing the best that we can."

"Yeah. I agree."

He couldn't believe he had a daughter. He still hadn't gotten used to the idea.

"If you don't mind, I'd like to go home."

"We haven't made it to the stable yet," he said, and then he shook his head. "But of course, I don't mind. Let's take a rain check on the stable for some other time?"

She nodded and began gathering their things up. There had been a change in her, and he wasn't sure exactly what it was. But she seemed...anxious.

Regardless, he helped her gather their things and then carried them as they headed back up the beach.

He wasn't sure how this new development was going to play out, but he did know that if he wanted to fix things, and he did, he needed to make sure that he was treating Dakota the way she deserved to be treated, but he wasn't sure exactly what that was.

Thankfully, he knew someone who did. He would spend a lot of time praying about this. Maybe God would show him whatever it was that he needed to know.

Because, like Dakota had just said, he'd messed up. But messing up wasn't the end. It was what he learned and what he did to fix it that mattered.

Chapter 10

Two days later, Dakota didn't feel any better.

The walk on the beach with Ryan had upset her in ways she hadn't known she even cared about.

But talking to him had made her realize that one of her daughters had a dad who was interested in her, and one didn't, and that could end up splitting her girls apart.

Her children fought just like normal sisters did, but maybe because of all of the hardship they'd been through, they were extremely close. Maddie as the elder was very protective and mothering of Rachel. Rachel was less agreeable, and possibly finding out that Maddie had a dad who lived close and really cared about her might be hard for her.

Both of them had expressed sadness when their father had left, of course. Rachel especially had sometimes cried inconsolably at night.

Dakota had tried counseling, but that hadn't seemed to make much difference. The counselor herself said that children make it through divorce because they have no choice. That they were resilient. That there wasn't a whole lot she could do other than support her daughters and encourage them and let them know that their mother loved them. After all, Dakota could hardly force her husband to want his children.

Added to that was the fact that she felt guilty for allowing him to think that both girls were his.

That wasn't something she wanted to face either, but she probably owed him an apology. Owed him the truth. Owed him...something.

And that irritated her, because he'd been the one who cheated, why was she the one who should apologize?

It didn't matter. If she hadn't treated him right, she needed to admit it.

She finished arranging the latest ship-
ment of items that she'd gotten on one
of the shelves that Ryan had put up the
day before.

He had been working in the showroom
all day, and she had managed to find
things to do in the residence. There was
plenty to do.

She was thankful that the girls had
school to go to, although they would be
out soon, and the summer tourist season would be upon them.

That thought alone made Dakota's
hands tremble. What if her store wasn't
a success? What if it failed? She already
had so many bills facing her, and she
didn't want to pay them, because she
didn't want to see the balance in her

bank account go down. Somehow having that money in there gave her a feeling of safety that she knew it shouldn't. Her security should be in her trust in God, but the temptation to trust in money in the bank was strong.

The apartment felt claustrophobic, and she had trouble drawing breath. Her anxiety had been getting worse.

Lord, I want to trust You, but I do need money. It's not an unreasonable fear, since I have two girls depending on me. Please help me to stay calm and to trust that You have a plan for me. Help me to see it.

Her prayer made her anxiety a little less sharp, but she still needed to get out. Taking another deep breath, she looked around the room to make sure there wasn't anything she forgot to turn off and then opened the door, going down the steps and stepping out the back.

Being outside made her feel a little better, but she didn't stop until she had walked past the buildings in town and over to the rail of the pasture that was just two hundred or so yards from her back door.

Horses always eased her anxiety, and being outside usually helped as well. There was just something about nature and admiring it that made her mind slow down and realize that this small moment in time was not the panic-inducing monster that it felt.

"There you are," a voice said, and Dakota startled, laughing nervously as she realized she sounded like she was out of breath when she said, "Hey."

"Were you jogging?" Lana said, coming over and leaning against the fence.

"No," she said, still sounding out of breath.

"I just wanted to see if everything was okay and that you were settling in. Business has been picking up at the bed-and-breakfast as the days get warmer, but I didn't want to neglect to check on you. Your grandmother and I were good friends."

"She talked very fondly about you. She treasured your friendship and was sad that she drifted away when she moved."

"I missed her. I was glad that no one moved into her spot. It wouldn't seem like the same store without your gram there. It feels very much like a part of her is here again with you."

"That's a huge compliment. Thanks." She tried to focus on their conversation, rather than the fear that had taken hold of her. What was she going to do? Everything was on her shoulders. It was all her. She had no safety net and nowhere to turn if this didn't work out. Her girls depended on her, and she didn't want to let them down. She didn't want them to remember their childhood with their mother as a failure, someone who couldn't even take care of them. How was she going to feed them?

Her thoughts raced.

"I can't imagine moving from a place I'd known all of my life into a new spot, trying to get started on my own, and not just on my own, but with two little girls depending on me. That must be...a huge leap of faith."

She didn't feel like she had faith. She felt like all she had was fear.

Talk to her. She has wisdom she can share.

Dakota resisted. To show fear was to show weakness. She didn't want to show weakness. She wanted to show strength. After all, that was how she was raised. If she fell off her horse, she got right back on. She didn't even admit that it hurt, or that she was afraid, or any kind of negative emotion. She had to be strong, she had to push herself.

She would never have won anything if she had given in to her fear.

Why was she giving in to it now?

And why was she afraid to talk about it?

She wasn't big on letting everyone in the world know all of the things she struggled with, but... Lana was so motherly and kind. And she went out of her way to walk across the open lot and meet Dakota beside the fence.

Surely that showed she cared.

Like she sensed Dakota's struggle, Lana just leaned against the fence, looking at the horses and quietly waiting.

"I'm scared," Dakota finally said, her voice hoarse and laced with fear. She felt like she was going to die. Was this what a panic attack felt like? Hammering heart, breath that wouldn't come, and a sense of doom, like something terrible was going to happen only she wasn't in any danger at all. At least no immediate danger.

"I don't think you'd be human if you weren't afraid," Lana said casually.

Dakota held onto the sound of her voice like a lifeline. It was calming, sweet, and comforting. "Sometimes I can work through my fear, but right now, I feel like it's got a hold of me, what happens if I can't make this work? I have nothing to fall back on."

"God provided this for you, didn't He?" Lana said.

"He did."

"He's somehow been taking care of you all of your life, hasn't He?"

"So far. I don't know why I'm so afraid that all of a sudden at some point, unexpectedly, He's going to yank the rug out from underneath me and no longer provide. I mean, I could end up in a homeless shelter. Or unable to get to one, and be actually homeless."

"I can guarantee you that the town of Strawberry Sands is not going to allow that to take place." There was a firmness in Lana's tone that hadn't been there before. It made Dakota lift her head and meet her eyes. They were twinkling, but her face was serious.

"I don't want to be a burden."

"Is that something to be afraid of?" Lana asked, her brows raised, her expression wise.

Dakota wished she had the years and experience and the wisdom that seemed to follow Lana around like an aura. "No. I know it's not anything to be afraid of, but I want to be able to make this work."

"And you will. If the Lord's in it. But sometimes He has things for us to go through, things that are hard, but… Somehow when we go through them with Him, they become easy. If we allow it."

"I'm holding on too tightly. Is that what you're saying?"

"I don't know if that's exactly what I'm saying, but sometimes we hold onto the things that we think should happen. That we expect. That we desire. And God has a different plan in mind. We get all upset and concerned and worried and fret about how things are going to work out the way we think they should, when we could just live a life of peace and ease if we allow God to have His way without us fighting Him every step of the way."

"You make it sound like I'm one of my children. Sometimes they just need to be quiet and relaxed and things will work out."

"Maybe that's why God refers to us so much as His children. I did the same thing when my kids were growing up. I would be disciplining them, and I would find myself saying things like, aren't you ever going to learn? And I would think that God could say the same thing to me, you know?" She laughed softly. "I tried to stop saying that to my kids, because God never said it to me."

"It's kind of hard for me to imagine you needing help," Dakota said. Her stomach was still a tight ball that felt like it was going to implode, but she was breathing easier.

"Oh, trust me, I had a lot of days of fear after my husband left. I had all these kids running around that were looking to me to feed them and clothe them and take care of them, and they thought I was a capable adult, when I felt like I was still just a young teen girl inside. I was in my thirties, but I didn't feel like that."

"That's me," Dakota said on a small laugh. "How did I get to be an adult? I don't feel like one. And I don't feel like I know how to do it. I need...a manual or something."

"God gave us the Bible. That must be all we need, since it's all He gave us. Although, normal people have parents. In a situation like this, you should have your mom to fall back on."

"I wish," Dakota said fervently.

"Let me be your mom."

Her eyes widened, and she looked at Lana. Was she serious?

"That's…nice but impractical. I can't just pretend you're my mom."

"Why not?" Lana asked, smiling. "Maybe that's why God sent me here. After all, I wanted to get out an hour ago, but I had a guest who came in and was telling me about the issues that she was having with her husband, and I wasn't able to come see you. And yet, the timing was perfect because here you were, and you were having a bit of a crisis if I'm not mistaken, mentally anyway, and God put me right here in front of you."

"I guess that's God showing that He's taking care of me, even as I was scared to death and panicking, God was orchestrating things so I would be taken care of." Dakota kind of murmured that to herself. After all, if it hadn't been Lana, if it had been someone else, she might not realize God was working things. There was something about Lana that seemed to point her toward Jesus.

"Anyway, I think that's probably true, and He put the thought in my head that I could be your mom. After all, I already have six kids, what's one more?" she said with a chuckle.

"But your kids are out of the house, self-sufficient, and this is your time to have for yourself."

"That's a bunch of hogwash. It's no more right to be selfish when you're old than it is when you're young. I can't just spend my days taking care of myself and making myself happy. I've got to find someone else to help, otherwise I'll be a waste. I don't want to waste these years. I want to use every single breath I have for Jesus. I don't think I will spend eternity regretting that. But I do think I'll spend eternity regretting it if I end up with a life of ease."

"If you're going to adopt me, you should adopt some foster children."

"I've been thinking hard about that. I just might."

Dakota raised her brows a little more. She hadn't heard too many people Lana's age talking about wanting to continue working. Usually, they looked forward to their retirement and a life of pleasure and low stress. They didn't consider that they could continue working for God and perhaps should.

"I don't see retirement mentioned in the Bible. Anywhere. In fact, God used Moses until it was time for him to go home. Then God took him. Same with Elijah. Same with Jesus. And Paul. Even John, on the Isle of Patmos, the last remaining disciple, God had a job for him. Somehow, we get old and we think that God can't use us anymore, but I say nothing could be further from the truth. I say God wants us to work until we're dead. When he takes me, then I'll know I'm done."

"That's an inspiring speech. I don't know why, but that actually helped my anxiety go away. I'm thinking less about what I need to do and more about giving my whole life to God. That... That actually does make me feel...free."

"The truth shall make you free. I think sometimes we struggle a little bit with that, but maybe the idea that God is in control, and that all we need to do is trust in Him, and that doesn't set us free, it makes us free. There's a difference."

Dakota had to admit she never noticed the difference. But from the way Lana talked, she assumed that people took the Bible verse and changed the word "make" to "set."

It was a subtle difference, but one that made all the difference. At least to her.

She didn't want to be set free, she wanted to be made free.

The anxiety that had been gripping her had faded. It was still there, she could feel it, but the idea that it wasn't all on her, that it was all on God, and all she had to do was trust and obey. So simple, a simple concept, but so hard for her to do. She wanted to take a hold of life and twist it to suit what she wanted.

"Is Ryan doing a good job?" Lana asked, changing the subject.

For a while, Dakota had almost forgotten that Ryan was Lana's son. "I suppose he is. I've been avoiding him."

"And why is that? Did he do something? Would you like me to talk to him?" Lana sounded truly concerned.

"No. He didn't do anything." How could she tell Lana that Ryan was the father of her child? That was Ryan's information to tell his mother, right?

Maybe. Maybe not, regardless, it wasn't information for today. She had to tell her daughter before she told anyone else. And she hadn't figured out an easy way to do that.

"I miss my horse," she said, not even realizing that she was going to say that. But finding out that it was true. "Always before when I have something to think about or a problem, I could go out, brush her, and... It sounds crazy, but I felt like she understood. I mean, obviously she never gave me any advice, I promise you."

Lana laughed. "I wasn't concerned that you were getting your advice from a talking horse, although if you had said that, I might be a little bit more concerned about your sanity."

"And rightfully so."

They grinned at each other, and Dakota found that just being reminded that God was in control, that whatever happened was part of His plan, and accepting that truth would make her free, had done wonders for her. Of course, if she was being honest, the fact that Lana had offered to be her mother and assured her that the town was not going to allow her to be homeless, or to fail, helped her, too.

"I have a tendency to want to have faith in my bank account. In the money there, and instead of trusting in God."

"I think we all struggle with that. But you know that God can add or take away from that money at any time."

"I know." Boy, did she ever. Especially when she had been taking care of her gram, there had been times when she hadn't known how she was going to buy food, then a neighbor would come by with a casserole, or a church member would drop off a gift card to the grocery store, or someone would bring a check by for work that she had done that she didn't even remember she hadn't been compensated for, and it was God taking care of her all of those times. It was funny how she forgot over and over again.

But maybe part of that stemmed from losing the foundation of having her grandmother there. Maybe she'd been putting some of her trust in people, rather than the Lord. When losing those people shook everything she knew and believed, she probably had been depending on them too much.

"Every experience you have, every time God comes through for you, it makes you a little wiser, a little more secure knowing that you can trust Him."

"I wish I were wise."

"I think that's one of those things that come with age. Don't wish it too fast, because youth fades, but I suppose I wouldn't trade anything that I had in my youth for the wisdom that I feel like I have now, although I suppose part of that is the wiser I feel, the less I feel like I know. If that makes sense."

"It's a paradox, but I think I understand. Sometimes it's better to not know what you don't know, because sometimes knowing that there is so much you don't know is scary."

"Not going to disagree with you there. But the solution is the same no matter what, to the fear anyway. God. And just knowing the truth that you can trust Him. That's what makes you free."

Dakota nodded, and they chatted for a bit more before she walked back to her apartment, completely in a different mind frame than she had been when she hurried out.

Talking to someone who was willing to share their wisdom had been priceless. But also holding onto the truth that she didn't have to stress, that she could just rest in God's plan, was even better.

Now, if she could just remember that and put it into use on a daily basis.

Chapter 11

Ryan gathered up his toolbelt and opened the door to his cottage. He had been walking to Dakota's shop, carrying his things that he didn't leave overnight. Dakota had been successfully avoiding him for the last three days, and he supposed that was for the best because he had no idea what he was going to say to her when he was actually able to talk to her.

He hadn't gotten any closer to a solution or ideas of what he could do to… He didn't even know. Be better friends?

He owed her so much, and he admired her. And the same feelings that he had for her from nine years ago had resurfaced.

If he was being honest, he wanted more. Or wanted to explore the possibility. And not just because she was the mother of his child.

Just the little bit of talking that he'd done with her, seeing the way she was, the kind of character she had, and her willingness to put herself aside in order to benefit someone she cared about, drew him like a magnet, and he couldn't resist.

Unfortunately, she didn't seem to have any trouble resisting him, if the way she'd avoided him for the last three days was any indication.

He took the back way to the store, wondering if maybe she would be outside, possibly getting a breath of fresh air or something. He didn't know where she spent her time. All he knew was that she didn't work in the shop until after he was gone.

But he could see as he came up over the small rise that there was no one around the back stoop on her building. But Griff stood outside the back door of the diner, his hands on the railing, looking up at the sky. He seemed to be taking a couple of deep breaths, maybe getting his bearings after the early morning breakfast rush.

"Good morning," Ryan said as Griff straightened and looked in his direction.

"Hey there. You've been working hard."

Ryan grinned. "I have. I actually like this kind of work. It's not the same as breaking horses, but it's good work. It's nice to see that you've accomplished something after a day, to be able to stand and look at it, you know?"

"Yeah. I like making a cake or watching people eat the food that I've made."

"Yeah, like that probably." Ryan had no idea about that. He could cook enough that he didn't poison himself usually, but he wasn't able to do anything fancy.

He'd been praying for a while that God would give him an idea of what he could do to convince Dakota that she should take a chance on him or at least allow him into her life, but he hadn't come up with anything.

Still, he found himself stopping in front of the low stoop and leaning against the railing opposite from where Griff leaned.

"I've seen Dakota look both ways before she steps out of her door. Do you have any idea why she'd be doing that?" Griff asked, and his words sounded casual.

Ryan snorted. "Maybe because she's looking for me?"

"Why would she be avoiding you? She scared?"

"I don't think so. But she's managed to avoid me the last three days I've been working there, so I'm guessing that there's something going on."

"And you don't have any idea of what?"

He could hardly admit that he was the father of her child. Beyond that, he had to shrug his shoulders. "I don't know."

But then, he added on, without really thinking about it, saying something he normally wouldn't. "I've actually been praying about how I can get her to trust me. She and I... We used to be pretty good friends, but then she ran into a little bit of trouble and I didn't help her. In fact, I let her down. And she... She made a pretty big sacrifice in order for me to be able to go on and do and accomplish the things I wanted to accomplish."

"Well. Did you know she was sacrificing at the time?"

"No. I just found out. And... I don't really know how to make it up to her."

Griff stood for a bit, his expression thoughtful as he seemed to study the sky. Finally, he pursed his lips, then said, "In my experience, a woman's usually pretty fond of her children. Anything you can do for the girls would probably help you win her heart."

"You think?" He was thinking that the one thing he needed to do was avoid the girls until she gave him permission to do something different.

"Sure. Take them horseback riding. Or... It's a nice breezy day, it would be a good day to go flying kites on the beach."

"Yeah. I always loved doing that." He probably could find some kites in his mom's basement if he went and looked.

"Of course, you could always invite Dakota to go along with you. You never know. She might accept."

"I doubt it. As much effort as she's put into avoiding me, I hardly think she's going to jump at the opportunity to spend extra time with me."

"Just make sure the girls have a good time. I mean, I wouldn't do it only as an ulterior motive. Dakota could use someone to help her, and the girls are lovable. My wife took over some food, and

Dakota acted like she really appreciated it. She's grateful to anyone who wants to help her, so I can't imagine that she'd turn you down."

"I guess I have a better imagination than you do," Ryan said, and there was a bit of sarcasm in his voice. He didn't have any trouble at all imagining Dakota telling him flat out that she didn't want him around.

"Or maybe you're just not as good at positive thinking as I am," Griff said, grinning a little, the sunlight shining off his bald head.

Was it positive thinking? Or was it that Griff could see what he couldn't?

Sometimes a person's experience helped them understand that the situation wasn't what it seemed.

"Do you have any other advice for me?" Ryan asked, figuring that if Griff was going to dish it out, he'd take it. He could use all the help he could get. After all, he'd managed to screw everything up. Big time. But seeing Dakota usually did that.

He couldn't help but wonder what would have happened if they hadn't been drinking the night of the championship. He knew for a fact they wouldn't have ended up sleeping together, and he wouldn't have a daughter right now. At least not one from that night.

Would they have figured out that they liked each other? They probably would have danced together regardless of the alcohol. Maybe that would have been the night that they realized that they meant more to each other than just friends. And he messed everything up.

"Be humble." Griff spoke, bringing Ryan back to the present.

"Simple, but extremely difficult sometimes."

"I know. Especially for men. We have a tendency to want to be in charge and not allow ourselves to look weak. Humility feels like weakness to us."

"Doesn't it ever." Ryan could attest to that. Winning a championship made him feel like he was on top of the world, and part of that was feeling like he was above everyone else, better than them. He liked that feeling, but he supposed that was just pride.

And yet he thought about the humility that Dakota had displayed when she had allowed him the freedom to win those championships. She was every bit as good of a barrel racer as he was of a bronc rider, but instead of insisting that she had to come out on top, she backed away and allowed him to win the accolades, while she won nothing. All she had was struggle. If the few things that his mother had said to him was any indication.

"Anything else?" he prompted when Griff didn't say anything for a while.

"Well, the fact that you're going to all this effort to impress her makes me think that there is a little bit more there than just a friendship thing."

"You could be right." He couldn't deny that. Although he didn't really want Dakota to know. She could use it against him... Except, someone who would back away and allow him to fly was hardly the kind of person who was going to hurt him in the long run. In fact, someone like Dakota was probably someone he could trust with anything.

Including his feelings, as uncomfortable as that was.

"Then I would say, if you feel that way, it's okay to let her know. Sometimes, when women know that you like them, they feel like there's nothing special about it, but Dakota doesn't seem like the kind of woman who wants a challenge. She seems like the kind of woman who wants stability and someone who's going to stick around for the long haul."

"Yeah. Too many people don't." Including her ex-husband.

"But she might be a little gun-shy."

"Yeah."

"Women like little gestures. It doesn't always have to be the big things. Although I think the idea behind the grand gestures is that you're not afraid to put the time and effort into impressing them. Or into making them smile. That you'll sacrifice what you want, and what makes you happy, in order for her to be happy. Somehow that really gets women."

"I see."

"I think gifts are good, they show that you are thinking of her."

Ryan snorted. All he did was think about Dakota. Pretty much for the last three days solid. And he hadn't come up with any of the things that Griff had.

"You know you can't account for human feelings, but if she's looking for someone solid and dependable, someone who will take care of her, someone who will make time for her, and take care of her girls, there are a lot of things you can do to show her you're that guy."

"I don't know why I couldn't think of these things on my own. But I couldn't," Ryan said. They seemed obvious now, and he could hardly wait to get started.

"But you know, all women are different. Maybe you could just ask her what she likes." Griff grunted, and then he straightened. "I better get back to work. My wife likes it when I do that." He grinned, then turned, and walked back into the diner, leaving Ryan standing at the rail, thinking hard.

He had been impressed with Dakota's sacrifice, but there was nothing that he could do that would match that. But thanking her for it seemed so...not good enough.

Chapter 12

Ryan pressed his lips together as he walked around the front of the shop, using the key his mother had given him to let himself in.

Dakota looked up from where she was working behind the counter that he'd installed, surprise on her face. There was a cash register sitting on it that hadn't been there the day before.

She glanced both ways before she backed slowly away.

"I didn't realize you were here," she said.

"I wasn't, not until I just walked in the door."

"Right," she said, tripping on something that was lying on the floor and catching herself before putting a hand on the wall.

"You okay?" he asked, hurrying forward. Knowing she wasn't on her deathbed. But using it as an excuse to get closer.

"Yeah. I'm fine."

"Are you sure?" he asked, feeling stupid. She tripped, caught herself before she hit anything, and used the wall to steady herself. Of course she was fine.

"Yeah."

"I wanted to know if it would be okay if I took the girls after school today?"

"Took them?" she asked, her voice breaking a little, her eyes widening in alarm.

"No. Not take them, take them. Just, you know, I wanted to take them and go fly kites or something."

"Both of them?"

"And you too if you want to come," he said, wondering where the husky note in his voice had come from.

She trembled a bit, and he put a hand on her arm.

"Are you sure you're okay?"

"I'm fine." But she took a deep breath, like she was trying to calm herself.

"Dakota, is there something up?"

"No. Why?"

"Because it seems like you're trying to avoid me?"

"Maybe I am." She lifted her shoulder. "Is that a problem?"

"I guess not. If that's what you want. But it's not what I want."

He dropped his hand and moved back. He had wanted to move his fingers up her arm, her skin was just as soft as he remembered, and move closer. But he didn't want to push her into something that she wasn't ready for. And she obviously wasn't ready for this.

"I have to go. I have, um, you know, things to do in the back."

He grunted. She was obviously coming up with some kind of excuse to get away from him.

"You didn't tell me if I could take the girls after school?"

"Sure."

"I... I need to dig up kites in my mom's basement. Maybe... Maybe we could go kite flying some other time, and I could take them for a horse ride this after-noon? Is that okay?"

"I'd like them to ride." She seemed to re-gain her equilibrium as she moved away from him. "I'd really like for them to be able to spend more time with horses. I..." Her voice trailed off, and he wondered again if she was going to talk about Goldie.

He never mentioned what he'd done, and... That would be a gift. He spent a lot of his down payment that he was expecting to be able to buy a ranch with, to buy her horse. It would be a huge sacrifice to give the horse back to her.

But she didn't have any place to keep it... He pushed the thought out of his head. Or maybe he tucked it away to think about some other time.

"All right then. Horses were a big part of your life. Mine too."

"Are you still training?" she asked. And he considered that a win, that she was trying to have a conversation with him.

"Yeah. I have three right now I'm working with. One that is almost ready for me to put up for sale."

"I'm sure you're really good at that."

"I hope so. I enjoy doing it."

"Maybe I can find someone else to work in here, so you can spend more time with them."

"No." His word was spoken immediately. He didn't want someone else to have this job. This was the only way he had an excuse to come see her.

But maybe coming to see her without an excuse was even better. Still, he would finish this job.

"You're doing good work. I'm sure the money that I had allotted for this has almost run out."

"No. I can't accept payment for this."

"I insist."

"And I insist on not. You're the mother of my child."

Her breath caught. He wanted to push her. Wanted to ask when she was going to tell her daughter that he was her father, but he didn't. He didn't want to push her away.

"I haven't said anything yet. And I'd appreciate it if you don't."

"I won't. Not until you say it's okay. Although, know that I want to."

"I know."

He nodded, figuring that was fair enough. "Are you sure you don't want to go riding with us?"

"I have too much work to do. That part of my life is over. I have to face it."

"It doesn't have to be. You can still enjoy a ride. I... I'm hoping to buy a ranch at some point, and..." What was he going to say? That she could live on it with him? Hardly. Not unless she was willing to marry him. Was that what he was angling for? He could barely get her to talk to him. There was no way that they would be getting married anytime soon.

Except with God, all things are possible.

Lord? I could use a little help if this is going to be possible.

He remembered that prayer later that afternoon, when the girls got home from school and he packed his things up. He'd talked to them as they walked through the front of the store each day on their way to the back where the living quarters were. It was obvious to him as he looked at Maddie that she was his child. She had his eyes and his chin. She had her mother's nose and her high cheekbones. Her hair was a mixture of their colors, lighter than Dakota's but darker than his.

She had his easygoing personality but Dakota's mothering instincts as she bossed her little sister around, sometimes with love, sometimes with force.

"Are you going to let us help you today?" Maddie said cheerfully as she walked in from school.

"Well, your mom said that we could go horseback riding if we wanted to. I was hoping that the two of you would come with me."

"I want to go!" Rachel said, never wanting to be left out. She wanted to do everything her older sister did, and there was a competitive streak in Rachel that reminded him of Dakota. She wanted to do everything better too.

It reminded him that Dakota giving up her career and the possibility of a championship for him was even more of a sacrifice than he wanted to let on. After all, her competitive nature would have driven her to be the best. But instead, she allowed him to be the best.

Maddie bit her lip. "I don't want to go without Mom," she said, and she threw a worried glance in the direction of the living area.

"I invited her to go too. She's welcome."

"I'll go ask if she'll go," Maddie said, running to the back.

Rachel chattered about how much she loved horses and about the pretty golden horse that her mom used to have.

He smiled as she described Goldie.

This didn't seem like the time to mention that Goldie lived right here in Strawberry Sands.

They'd be going to his brother Matt's stable, who had beginner horses that the girls could ride with ease. They wouldn't be seeing Goldie, but he smiled knowing that Dakota's daughters loved the horse as well.

A plan began to form in his head.

He talked with Rachel some until Dakota appeared in the doorway, Maddie beside her, her arm around her waist.

"I'm not sure that Maddie's going to go. Are you okay just taking Rachel?" She said the words with an uptilt to her chin and a look that said that she figured that he wasn't going to want to, but she couldn't say why out loud.

"I sure am. But Maddie said she hoped you'd go."

"I don't think I can." She kind of stumbled, and he figured it was because she didn't want to go with him.

"It might be good for you. You know, you've been working pretty hard. It would be good for you to take a little time off. It's a beautiful day out. And... You know you miss riding."

Her eyes narrowed a bit at the intimate way he spoke. Of course he knew that she missed riding. Anyone who was born to be on a horse the way she was would miss it.

"I'd really like it if you'd go," he said, not sure whether that would convince her or drive her away.

"Please, Mommy?" Maddie said, squeezing her mom tighter but looking up with pleading in her eyes.

"I guess. But we can't stay long. I do have a lot of work to do."

"Maybe you could ride with us, and then the girls and I can get dessert at the diner, of course… If you want to do that with us, you could."

"Maybe but most likely not," Dakota said.

"Mommy. I like it when you do things with us."

"I like doing things with you too, kiddo," Dakota said with a smile and a squeeze.

"I just like to ride horses," Rachel said, jumping up and down.

"You guys need to go change out of your school clothes, and I'll talk to Mr. Ryan."

Ryan figured by the sound of that that he was in big trouble, but he didn't allow that to worry him. At least she had agreed to go, and her daughters seemed excited. As far as he could see, he was winning.

Chapter 13

"So you want to hold the kite in this hand, and hold your string in the other hand, and then run along the beach." Ryan held the kite up as an example, with the string in the other hand, as he spoke earnestly to Rachel.

Rachel had been determined to get her kite in the air, but so far, she had had no success. Dakota had forgotten that there was a bit of a knack to flying kites. She'd been doing it for so long, since the breeze that blew off Lake Michigan was perfect for kite flying, that she forgot that she actually had to learn.

It was like riding horses.

Her girls had had so much fun with Ryan for the past two weeks. He'd taken them horseback riding several times. They'd gone for walks along the lake, and on one especially warm day, they'd even gone swimming. This was the first time they'd flown kites. It turned out there were no kites left in his mother's basement, and he had to buy new ones.

Dakota had wanted to stock them in her store, because it was something that the tourists would purchase, and so he waited for her order to come in.

The girls' last day of school had been today, and they had celebrated by going to the beach.

Monday would be her grand opening. It was also the official first day of summer vacation and the unofficial start of the tourist season.

She had a lot riding on it, but ever since her talk with Lana, she had a peace about it.

She just hoped that God knew what He was doing.

She thought that a little sarcastically. Of course He did. She supposed what she really hoped was that He wasn't going to take her through anything that was especially difficult. She felt like she'd already been through a lot of difficult things.

Ryan ran along the beach, trying to get his kite in the air, and then, just as she thought it was going to catch, it went up, flipped, and went straight down and did a nosedive into the sand.

Maddie and Rachel both laughed, while Ryan stood there with his hands on his hips, shaking his head with a smile on his face.

There was no doubt that everyone was having fun.

As Dakota had the last two weeks. She hadn't gone with Ryan every time he'd taken her girls, and he hadn't taken them every single day, but they definitely spent a lot of time together, and it was past time that they told Maddie about her father.

She appreciated the fact that Ryan had given her plenty of time to come to grips with that.

Now, her prayer was that Maddie would be happy and not worried, since Maddie had her own tendency toward anxiety.

She didn't want to model that for her children, and seeing it in her daughter made her double her efforts to trust God and not allow her fear to win out over her faith.

"Watch me!" Rachel said, running by where her sister was trying to get her kite out of the sand without breaking it. Her own kite was in the air, her little legs churning as fast as they would go.

The feel of the sun on her face, the breeze from the lake, the fresh air, and the laughter she was sharing with people she loved made Dakota's heart warm as she watched her daughter try with all her might to get her kite to fly.

It was a day to remember for the rest of her life. Her girls would grow up, her life would change, but she would have these beautiful memories tucked deep in her heart. Just a month ago, she might not have thought she'd ever have good memories again, but... Ryan had pulled her out of that place and shown her that while they were working on getting her store ready, they could still have fun.

He'd taken her girls and won their hearts.

She appreciated that more than she could say. She smiled as Ryan clapped his hands and encouraged Rachel as her kite caught the air current and soared.

But her legs must have grown tired, because she slowed just a bit, and her kite dropped.

It didn't nose plant quite as hard as Ryan's had, but it still lay sadly on the sand as Rachel came to a stop.

"You know, I seem to recall that your mother is pretty good at this. Maybe she'll show us how it's done."

"I recall several times that you needed my help to get your kite in the air. Maybe I should be the one teaching you how to fly," Dakota said, with plenty of humor in her voice. She did seem to recall that he had been terrible at flying kites, and it was something she was good at. But she was sure that he had figured it out eventually. It would be almost impossible to live beside the lake and not be an expert at kite flying.

"Bet Mom can get her kite up first," Rachel said, holding her hands on her hips.

"And I bet she can't," Ryan said, lifting his brows and rising to her challenge. "If your mother wants to rise to the challenge, I can prove it."

"Okay," Rachel said, looking skeptical.

"You can borrow mine, Mommy," Maddie said, walking over and offering Dakota her kite.

Dakota took it with a smug look that she didn't quite feel. Ryan might have been terrible when they were younger, but she hadn't flown a kite in years and didn't know if she remembered how.

"It seems like he needs me to show him how this is done," Dakota said, lifting a brow, as she wound the string up to a length she was comfortable with.

It felt familiar under her hands, even if it had been more than a decade since she'd flown one.

"I think if you lose, you need to go to church with me tomorrow," Ryan said. "After all, we can hardly have a challenge without the winner getting something."

"And an appropriate prize is me going to church with you?" Dakota said, humor in her tone. That wasn't exactly what she would have guessed he would have suggested.

"Yeah. That's actually a really good prize," Ryan said, and all the humor had fled. She was close enough that she could hear his low tone and hear something that underlay it. She wasn't quite sure what.

But he'd had moments of seriousness every time they'd been together. Like he wanted more. More than just laughter and fun. More than just her as a mom coming with her girls...like he wanted her.

She didn't want him to know that he actually made losing seem like a good possibility. In fact, she found herself entertaining the thought that she might lose on purpose, just to allow him to get the prize. But there was a competitive streak in her that would not allow her to give up that easily.

She lifted her chin and gave him a superior look, which was a little difficult considering that he was taller than she was. "Challenge accepted."

She glanced over at Maddie. "You can tell us when to start."

Maddie grinned, and Rachel sidled up to her, like she wanted to have a part in it too.

Dakota looked at her younger daughter. "You can tell us who wins."

"You do, Mommy," she said easily.

Dakota and Ryan both laughed together, and Dakota stuck her nose even further in the air. "There you go. I won. Easiest contest ever."

Instead of rolling his eyes and telling Maddie to go ahead and start them, he shrugged. "All right. What's your price?"

He surprised her. That's all she could think, because the words came out of her mouth without thought. "You go to church with me."

He barked out a laugh. "Nicest consolation prize ever."

And that was another one of those statements that he made; his eyes were twinkling, but there was a serious tone underlying his words that she loved.

"You mean you're not really going to fly a kite?" Rachel asked, disappointment making her words sound sad.

"Of course we are." Dakota lifted her brows at Maddie.

"On your mark, get set, go!" she said, barely waiting for Dakota and Ryan to get set.

Dakota took off faster than he did, since he was still winding string, but he caught up soon enough.

"Get away from me. You're going to get your string tangled up with mine!" She laughed as she ran.

"Seems like you run, and I follow you. It doesn't matter where you're going," he said, and maybe it was a good thing that they were running, because she couldn't stop and study him and try to figure out what exactly those words meant.

Did that mean...he wanted to follow her? That was new. It seemed like before, he couldn't wait to get rid of her.

She knew he had apologized for that, and she believed him that he was sorry. But sometimes when a person was sorry that didn't necessarily mean that they were going to change anything. Or it didn't always mean that they felt like there was anything to change.

Ryan seemed to be turning over a new leaf.

She liked it and appreciated his consideration.

But that did not mean that she was going to allow him to win. It had been a long time, but the handling of the kite came back. She could feel the wind tugging, tell which direction it was going, and knew which way to pull the string in order to point the kite where it needed to go.

She'd spent hours with Ryan along the shore flying kites. It was something that kept them out of trouble. And she knew her gram preferred her to do that over riding horses, which always scared her gram. She hadn't grown up around them, and she didn't understand Dakota's deep and abiding love for them.

But it looked like Ryan hadn't lost any of his muscle memory either, since his kite was no lower than hers.

She let out more string, and the wind picked up, pulling the string, and lifting her kite.

But as the breeze was wont to do next to the lake, in the next instant it switched directions, and her kite tilted crazily, while Ryan's stayed high in the air.

He looked over at her and laughed, shouting, "Looks like you've lost your touch!"

The words had no sooner left his mouth than his kite lifted and pitched and turned down, making a diagonal line toward the lake.

Everything might have been okay, but as Ryan raced to get to the right angle to steady his kite, she lost sight of him, trying to fix her own, and in the next heartbeat, he brushed by her.

That might have been okay too, except her leg was going back, their feet got tangled, and they both ended up on the sand with her a little bit on top of him.

"You're a little heavier than you used to be," he said.

"I'm pretty sure I'm supposed to get mad when some fella says something like that to me."

"You're not going to get mad. You never do."

He was right. She got her feelings hurt sometimes, but she never got mad. Not at Ryan. And typically not at much else. She didn't know why, she just didn't have a temper.

She had other issues, like anxiety, lack of trust in the Lord, and a weakness for a man with deep blue eyes and the ability to set her heart racing with just a look.

"Maybe I started," she said, forgetting for a moment that she had two girls who were a hundred yards down the beach waiting for her to put a kite in the air and expecting her to get up.

His arms went around her, and his fingers touched the small of her back, moving just a little, enough to let her know that they were there.

She was tempted to run her hands through his hair, to touch the stubble on his face, to lower her head toward his.

"I'm sorry. I didn't mean to run into you."

"Not only does she not get mad, she apologizes when it was my fault."

"Well, you aren't apologizing, and I figured that one of us should."

"Always wanting to get along."

"There's nothing wrong with that."

"No. There's not. I actually admire it. Sometimes I'm too eager to fight, more eager to make sure the other person knows that they're wrong than I am to extend grace. You've always been a good influence on me in that way."

"Maybe I'm not like that anymore."

"I don't really see how you've changed at all, except maybe to get better." His voice dropped on those last few words, and it made her stomach tingle and the hairs on her neck curl.

She hated that she had that reaction, but she also loved it at the same time if that was possible.

"Dakota, I—"

"No."

Chapter 14

Dakota didn't know what Ryan was going to say, but she didn't want to hear it. Whatever it was in his eyes, whatever he was saying with his fingers on her back, the tone of his voice, she couldn't take it. She had too many other things she had to deal with, she couldn't go through this with Ryan again.

"You don't even know what I was going to say."

"I don't have to know. I don't want to go there."

"Go where?" And he sounded truly baffled, like he didn't know what she was talking about, or more likely, he didn't know how she knew what he was talking about.

"Anywhere. Whatever you're thinking, I don't want to have anything to do with it. I can't."

"What do you mean you can't?" he asked, lifting his head a little off the sand like changing angles would allow him to look at her and see her better.

"I mean, I've already gone down this road once with you, and it hurt."

"I promise. This time won't hurt."

"You can't promise that."

"It will be different than last time."

"How?" she asked, wishing that she didn't even bother. He could make promises all he wanted to, but she had a man stand beside her in front of a preacher and make promises, and he hadn't bothered to keep them.

That man wasn't Ryan. He never made her any promises that he hadn't kept. The night that they'd spent together there hadn't been any promises exchanged.

"Aren't we a little older? A little wiser?"

"I think I'm just as dumb as I ever was," she said, knowing she should push herself away and get up, and yet she didn't.

Out of the corner of her eye, she could see that her girls had been distracted by something along the shore of the lake, and they were both squatted down and looking at it. At least they were okay. She half wished they'd run and interrupt them, because she didn't want to move.

"You're not. You've learned a lot in the years that we've been apart, and you were always smarter and wiser than me anyway."

"No. If I were wiser, I'd be up by now. Why aren't I?" she asked, emphasizing the words but not looking at him, because she was asking herself.

"Maybe because you feel it too."

"I feel nothing." Such a lie. She didn't even try to make it sound true.

"Saying it doesn't make it true."

"I know. I want it to be true."

"But it's not."

She didn't answer, even though it was more of a statement than a question. To her dismay, she felt her eyes pricking, and she pulled her lips in between her teeth. She would not lie here and cry.

"No. Don't," he said, and one of his hands came off her back, pushing her hair back from her face and gently cupping her cheek with his big hand. "I don't want to watch you cry. Not ever again."

"You've never seen me cry," she said, and just those words made her suck the tears back. She would not let him see her cry. Would not.

He was quiet for a minute, then he said, "When we were kids, it didn't matter how badly you got hurt, you didn't cry. But…" He swallowed. "The night we were together, you did. You told me it was a good cry."

She shook her head. "I don't remember."

"Don't, or don't want to?" he asked, and he lifted his brows, tilting his head and trying to meet her eyes.

She refused.

There were foggy memories from that night. She wanted to think that they were all obliterated by the alcohol that she consumed, as though that somehow let her off the hook for the way she acted that night, and the things she allowed to happen, the things that she did. The things she encouraged.

"I don't want to talk about that." Ever. She didn't ever want to talk about that.

"Not talking about it doesn't make it not happen."

"Don't you think I know that? There's a little girl over there that reminds me every single day of what happened that night."

"A little girl I love."

"I love her too," she said, just as fierce as she had been speaking, even though his words had pulled the anger right out of her.

"There. You're angry," he said, smiling and allowing one of his fingers to trace down her cheek.

"Not anymore."

"Short-lived. I like it."

"I'm still right though. It's no good. None of it is any good."

"Can't we build something together? You and me. Along with the girls." He sounded like he was pleading with her, and she knew if she stayed there, he'd talk her into whatever castles in the sand he was building. She didn't want sandcastles. She wanted a reality. She wanted a solid life. Dependability. Someone who wasn't going to go chasing after the next championship or the next girl that caught his fancy.

Although, if she were being honest, Ryan chased after the first but never the second.

"Let me go," she said, even though he wasn't really holding her.

He dropped his hand immediately, and disappointment crossed his face. "Dakota, tell me what you want. Please. What will it take?"

"I don't know," she said, and that was honest. She really didn't know. Didn't know if she could ever go back into a relationship.

"I was always a good friend," he stated, and she had to agree.

"You were."

"And you are the best friend I ever had."

"I'm sorry." She laughed a little. If she was the best friend he ever had, he was sure lacking in the friends department.

"Don't be." He smiled a little, but his look was sad.

She pushed up, offering her hand as they used the leverage between them to stand to their feet. "I guess neither one of us are going to church tomorrow."

"Or both of us are going, and we're each going with each other."

She laughed. Shaking off the melancholy that had descended upon her. Thoughts about what might have been. Thoughts about what was. About the memories that she'd suppressed for a long time. Things she didn't want to face about herself. But she felt like he was right. She was wiser than she used to be.

They walked over, picking up their kites and figuring out how to untangle the strings. It wasn't hard, and they set to work getting the kites in the air again. This time staying far enough away from each other that there was no chance of them getting tangled up together.

Fifteen minutes later, they had their kites flying high and walked back over to the girls who had found an interesting piece of driftwood and had used it to start making a house in the sand.

The girls were so intent on what they were doing that they were shocked to turn and see them coming back with the kites up.

"I can see we're going to be teaching this again," Ryan said as the girls jumped up peppering them with questions about how they did it.

"Yay! That means we'll be coming to fly kites again," Maddie said happily, like she had been concerned that this would be the only time she would ever go kite flying with her mother and Ryan.

They handed the kites off to the girls and stood side by side, watching them run down the beach with them flying in the air.

"I'd really like to tell her," Ryan said.

"Then let's do it today," Dakota replied. They might as well. Waiting wasn't solving anything. All it was doing was giving her a bit of a reprieve. And she had enough of a reprieve. He'd been patient, waiting on her, not pushing, not asking, and not trying to force her hand. The very least she could do was to allow him to finally tell his daughter that she was his.

"What about Rachel?" he asked. "What do you want me to say to her?"

She was tempted to tell him to tell both of her girls that he was their dad, but... What was that going to mean for them?

"I know that you have a lot on your plate, and I'm kind of pushing you a lot today, but I'd really like to be a dad to both of them."

She nodded her head. "I know." She took a deep breath, pushing the anxiety that wanted to consume her aside.

Lord? I don't know what to do. I want to rest in Your plan, but I don't know what that is. Can You show me?

That she left in her head, because right in front of her was God showing her, the man.

"I don't know how to explain it, because there might come a point where Rachel's dad actually does want to be a part of her life, but for now, she doesn't have anyone. And whatever you say to Maddie, I appreciate you including Rachel as well."

"Then let's play it by ear. I don't know how to explain, but I guess my main concern is making sure that I do whatever is best for the girls."

"The best thing for the girls would be for their mother to have made smarter decisions, but there's nothing I can do about that now." Much to her regret.

Why did she have to wait until she was older to actually be wise enough to make decisions that would help her daughters become what they needed to be, not hurt them?

"It's okay. Whatever we do, we'll work it out."

He might not have been able to read her mind, but he could read her face, and she appreciated him trying to alleviate her concerns.

"Thank you. I... I'm starting to feel like you might be too good to be true."

"No. Not too good at all. I... I do have something I want to talk to you about."

"Now?"

"No. Maybe not until we get a little bit of time alone. Where we're not going to be interrupted."

She couldn't imagine what in the world he wanted to talk to her about. They'd already basically decided that they were going to have a relationship. At least that's what she thought they decided while they were lying on the sand back there, but she supposed they didn't exactly use those terms.

By that time, the girls had run down the beach and had stopped and started back a little slower.

Their faces were red, their hair wind-blown, and they looked so healthy and happy.

"They look so carefree," Dakota said, wishing that they really were.

"I think they are. I think they feel secure. They know their mother loves them, and they had a fun day. What more could a kid want?"

"Family that's not blown up," she said, hating the bitterness in her tone but not knowing how to fix it.

"And maybe that'll happen someday. Someday soon," Ryan said as the girls ran up to them.

She couldn't answer him, but she wouldn't have known what to say anyway. She wanted to deny it and to argue, but should she? Or was this really what the Lord wanted for her?

Maybe she'd just been alone so long she couldn't believe that there would be a happy ever after for her.

Regardless, she helped the girls as they pulled the kites down and folded them up.

"I was hoping I could talk to you about some things. Do you guys have a few minutes for me?" Ryan asked the girls as they laughed and giggled and barely had the kites down before they wanted to see if they could put them back up themselves.

"Can we fly kites after you're done?" Maddie asked, smiling.

Dakota's heart felt so warm and happy to see her daughter enjoying herself.

And giggling. Maddie could be such a serious worrywart.

"If it's okay with your mom. Although I'm getting hungry."

"Me too!" Rachel said, rubbing her stomach.

Dakota rolled her eyes. Rachel was always hungry. She couldn't even imagine what the girl would be like as a teenager.

"All right, let's go here and sit down."

Dakota, her heart in her throat, met Ryan's eyes. He was serious, but there was an excitement about him that she wished she had. Instead, she just felt dread. This had the potential to rock all of their worlds.

Lord. You can make this go the exact right direction. Please.

She didn't close her eyes, but she followed her girls over and sat down, hoping that this wasn't the worst mistake of her life.

Chapter 15

Ryan knew he should be nervous. He really didn't have any idea what he was going to say, but he was excited. The girls liked him, enjoyed his company, and had fun with him. They listened to him, and that was probably more Dakota than anything, because they were good girls.

But if he handled this right, and if Dakota was going in the direction he thought she was, slowly moving toward him, he could end up with a ready-made family.

He swallowed. He hadn't thought he was a family man, but he'd come a long way from the days of not wanting to have anything to do with a wife and kids, thinking they would hold him back, keep him down, and keep him from achieving his dreams.

Those dreams didn't mean anything. It was people. Family. The folks who sacrificed in order to see him fly.

He wanted to spend his life with those people. With Dakota. With her daughters. Their daughters.

He tried to calm himself down, because he had a lot riding on this.

The girls sat down in the sand, then he knelt in front of them.

Dakota knelt down a little off to the side and behind the girls so that their focus could be on him.

It was so much like her. Not taking the spotlight, not trying to control anything, but being there, his wingman. Supporting him, available if he needed her, but ready to yield the spotlight, and whatever else she had to in order to help him be what he needed to be.

He wanted to tell her right then and there that he loved her. It had almost slipped out earlier.

Just like he'd almost bent his head and kissed her as well. But he didn't think he wanted to kiss her until she knew that he loved her, and maybe not even until he knew that she loved him back. After all, he wasn't in the habit of kissing just anyone. He didn't go around with his goal in life being to get kissed or to kiss. His goal in life was far more than just a kiss. He wanted everything. But only from Dakota.

"Are you going to die?" Maddie asked, her brows furrowed.

"Are you leaving?" Rachel asked.

He shook his head at both of their questions. "I want to be your dad."

Well, that was one way to say it. He supposed that was what he got for wanting to have this talk before he thought about what he was going to say.

"You mean like live with us?" Maddie asked, tilting her head and slanting her gaze at her mom.

"Maybe eventually," he said, smiling at the horrified look on Dakota's face. That wasn't the direction she wanted this to go, but he'd known all along that was the direction he wanted.

"Why not now?" Rachel asked.

"Well, a man isn't supposed to live with a woman when they're not married. At least that's what the Bible says. And I wouldn't want to do that to your mom."

"Then get married," Maddie said easily. Like it was that simple.

"Maybe we will. But in the meantime, I... Your mom and I were together a long time ago, before your mom met the man she married. The man who became your dad."

This was harder than he thought it was going to be.

"And because you're older," he looked at Maddie, "your mom was pregnant with you before she got married to Gregory, Rachel's dad."

Maddie sat still, but her face scribbled up, and her eyes narrowed. "She was pregnant before she was married to Dad?"

It irritated him to hear her call someone else her father. But he pushed that irritation aside. "Yeah. That means that I'm your dad."

He wasn't sure he needed to explain it in any greater detail, and he wasn't going to if Maddie would accept that.

"So Dad isn't my dad, but you are?"

"Yeah."

"What about me?" Rachel piped up, jumping up and putting her hand on his shoulder. "I want you to be my dad too."

"And that's fine with me. I want you to be my daughter. I... I don't know if I can adopt you eventually, but I'd like to."

"Adopt? Like... Like Rich and Kayla were adopted?" Maddie leaned around her sister and looked at her mom.

Her mom nodded. "Just like that."

It wasn't quite like that, since Maddie was actually his daughter, but he didn't think that she was at the age where he could exactly explain everything else.

He supposed through the years, there'd be more questions, and this was almost an anticlimax, because it had been so... He didn't want to say easy, but nondramatic.

He hadn't thought to ask Dakota whose name was on the birth certificate, but if Gregory didn't know, he was assuming that it was Gregory's name. But it was possible that Gregory would give up his parental rights, and Ryan actually could adopt both girls. That would be perfect, especially if Dakota allowed him to be more to her than just a friend.

He didn't want to get the cart ahead of the horses.

"Is that all you want?" Maddie asked, looking at kites.

"Yeah. That was it. I just was hoping that I could be your dad."

"Okay," Maddie said, shrugging her shoulder like it didn't matter.

"I want you to be my dad too," Rachel said, and he laughed, shaking his head. "But I think you got to marry Mom."

"All right." He lifted a brow at Dakota, then figured that it couldn't hurt to get all of the ammunition he could on his side. "We'll talk her into it. Because I'm willing."

"I'm not marrying anyone who doesn't love me." Her words were said softly but firmly.

"Can we fly kites?" Maddie asked, standing to her feet and looking at the neatly folded kites on the sand.

"Sure," Dakota said after meeting his gaze for a minute just to make sure that it was okay, and he wasn't going to die of hunger or something, apparently.

The girls picked up the kites and walked a little bit away.

"I could tell you that I love you, but I'd rather show you," he said, not forgetting what she had said before the girls had interrupted about the kites.

"I think that's probably the only kind of love I'm interested in. Love that has a little bit of action behind it. Seeing the other kind, it's just words and empty promises, and I'm not interested in that."

"And I wouldn't want that for you," he said, meaning it.

"All right then."

"We still on for church tomorrow?"

His question made her smile, as he intended, and she nodded. He offered his hand, and they stood together.

Maybe he should have let go of it, but he didn't, liking the way it felt in his and holding on to it.

She didn't try to pull away, and that made his heart smile.

Maybe there was some hope for them after all.

Chapter 16

Everything was ready for the big grand opening on Monday morning. Even if it hadn't been, Dakota wouldn't have skipped church. There were some things she couldn't live without and God was one of them. That was a lesson she had to learn as she aged, since it wasn't necessarily one she knew when she was younger.

"Did you change your shoes?" she called in to Rachel.

"I did, but I like the other ones better." Rachel's look was sullen as she walked out of her room in the nicer shoes Dakota had requested she change into. If this was how she was at six, Dakota could only imagine how she would be as a teen.

Was it something she was doing wrong? Could she be a better parent? A better mother?

A knock sounded at the door, firm and confident and she had no doubt it was Ryan.

Wouldn't it be nice to have him beside her as she tried to parent her girls?

She wasn't sure where that thought came from, but it was a comforting one. One she loved and that made her heart warm without her really thinking about it. One that felt surprisingly perfect and right.

He'd been so good with the girls over the past couple of weeks. They loved him even though he wasn't a pushover and didn't allow them to do whatever they wanted.

"I'll get it!" Rachel called, running to the door.

"Mommy said you'd be early," she said as she opened the door.

"And am I?" he asked, shooting a grin over her head at Dakota, whose heart seemed to flip and flutter, although she couldn't figure out why. It was just Ryan. The man whom she'd been friends with for years. Who had been hanging around, working in the store downstairs and spending time with her girls and her for the past few weeks. Just Ryan.

But that grin. And the way he chatted now with Rachel, telling her the time from his phone and listening to her say her mother was right. The way she knew he'd be early, that he'd arrive in a good mood, that he'd be kind and thoughtful, always.

He was the kind of man she could depend on. The kind who wouldn't walk away from her, nor his child. Who would adopt a little girl who wasn't his, just so she'd have a dad, too.

Her heart wanted to melt at her thoughts. She couldn't afford to get mushy and sappy before church. Although there was a part of her that asked why not? After all, Ryan seemed like he wanted more, had hinted yesterday that he did, had almost kissed her. He's said he wanted to show her he loved her.

Wasn't that what he'd been doing?

"Dakota?" he said, concern touching his face as he closed the distance between them, and she realized that she'd been daydreaming and had missed a question.

"I'm sorry. I was thinking. What did you say?" she asked, sticking a big smile on her face and trying not to show that her hands were sweating and her heart wouldn't stop acting like she'd never seen Ryan before.

"I rendered you speechless," he teased.

"You do look nice," she said, and she couldn't quite match his teasing tone. Because he did look nice, no, strikingly handsome, in his dark jeans and button up, with his cowboy boots and enough stubble on his chin to make her heart beat faster, if it hadn't been already.

"You are beautiful. Our girls get their looks from their mom, that's for sure."

The girls beamed. Dakota didn't miss that he'd called them "our" girls. Their eyes met and she felt like he noticed that she noticed and they were both okay with it.

"I know we were planning on a picnic this afternoon, but my mom wanted to know if you'd allow the girls to go to her house this afternoon. She's watching some of her other grandkids - my brother's kids - and was hoping our girls would come play as well. Mom loves a house full of children." He smiled at the girls. "I think she was hoping you girls would help her bake cookies."

"I love to bake cookies!" Maddie said, jumping up and down.

"Me, too!" Rachel echoed. Dakota's heart squeezed, since Ryan was including both girls. Either he'd told his mother that they were together, or she'd picked up on that herself. Whatever it was, Dakota couldn't imagine a family treating her girls and her any better.

"Is that okay?" Ryan asked as they made their way to the door.

"Yes." Of course it was. How could she turn that invitation down when her girls were so excited about it?

"I'd still like to spend the afternoon with you, if you're okay with it," he said in a voice lowered to a point where the girls couldn't hear as they filed out the door and down the stairs.

She stopped as she walked by him, breathing in his scent, clean and fresh, reminding her of character and strength and confidence. She wanted to stop and put a hand on his chest, look up into his eyes and...she wasn't sure what. Just knew she didn't want to walk by without touching him.

"I'd like that." She forced herself to walk forward, going down the stairs and following her girls out of the door. She should have declined. She had a big, grand opening in the morning. But everything was ready. There was nothing to do. Why not spend a last afternoon with Ryan before the stress of work and busyness of the tourist season descended upon them?

She couldn't really think of any reasons to decline as they walked around the building and up the sidewalk to the small church, even though she thought she should. Mostly because Ryan was too good to be true. She was going to lose her heart to him, and then where would she be?

Right where God wanted her, a voice in her head insisted. But sometimes she had trouble deciding what God wanted and what she wanted.

They arrived at the church before she could untangle that in her head and she put it aside to think about later. Ryan hadn't even been on her radar when her Gram passed away. It seemed like her world had come crashing down, but Ryan had arrived like a knight in shining armor. Was that really too good to be true? Or was it the Lord working in her life?

"Ryan, come give me a hand moving a few tables from the storage shed." Ryan's brother Matt jerked his head at her in greeting, but he motioned for Ryan and strode away without waiting for his brother to answer, as though confident in his help.

"Is that okay?" Ryan asked her, as her girls crowded close, the strange faces and new experience making them shy.

"Yes. Go right ahead. I'm going to find the Sunday School classes for my girls."

"They're both downstairs with Sally." He told her where the stairs were once she stepped in the front doors, and gave directions to their classroom. "I asked my mom early this morning before I left, so I could help you out." His grin said he was pretty proud of himself for thinking of them, and she had to admit, she appreciated his thoughtfulness.

"Thank you." She supposed her look was slightly besotted, but she couldn't get her face to do anything else as she met his eyes before he walked away, swinging his arms with a confident stride she remembered from years ago.

She wanted to stand and watch him, but her girls pressed closer, grabbing her hands and seeming like they weren't going to let her out of their sight.

"Come on, girls. Let's see if we can make some new friends today," she said, as she pulled her eyes away from Ryan and headed toward the church doors.

Several people greeted her as she walked in and went down the stairs, following Ryan's directions to Sally's classroom. She'd not met Sally before, but she assumed the friendly-looking woman who was about her age, who was directing children to take a few extra minutes to study their memory verse was the teacher.

"Hi! You must be Dakota. I'd heard you were coming with your girls."

"You have good informants."

"My spies are everywhere," she winked as she bent over introducing herself to Dakota's girls. She directed them to a pile of stickers and told them they could choose whichever one they wanted to put on the attendance chart.

"I didn't introduce myself. I'm Sally," Sally said as the girls skipped away, holding hands.

Dakota took her hand and shook it. "You already know my name."

"Ryan's mom told me he was bringing you today. I'm excited to meet you. Ryan deserves a great girl." Her smile was a little sad, as though she wanted to be someone's girl. Or maybe Dakota was being fanciful, since the idea that she might be just the girl for Ryan made her happier in a way she wasn't expecting.

"Teacher! I want this sticker!" a little boy called.

"Duty calls," Sally said, her bright smile back in place.

"Do you need help?" Dakota had to ask. There were a lot of kids and Sally was the only adult.

"Nope. I'll have these little ones in hand," she said with confidence. Dakota didn't argue, just nodded, thinking Sally seemed like a woman she would like to be friends with.

She waved good-bye to Sally. Her girls seemed to have totally forgotten about her existence, since they were bent over the pile of stickers with three other sweet little heads, chattering and smiling.

There was a small tug on Dakota's heart. She wasn't upset that her girls did so well without her, but more that they were growing up. Life was changing. Her gram was gone, she had moved to a new town and everything seemed new and slightly scary.

She swallowed. This was where her faith was supposed to see her through. Being sure that she knew she was doing what

God wanted her to do, and having faith that He would take care of her whatever happened.

She smiled at the people who greeted her, all the while saying a quick prayer that she would trust in God and consider this an adventure and not something that terrified her. After all, so far God had not let her down, had actually brought Ryan back into her life.

And Lana.

She'd barely thought that, when a soft, warm hand landed on her arm. "Dakota. Did Ryan remember to ask you if your girls could come to my house this afternoon?"

"He did. Are you sure it's okay? It won't be too much?"

"I'm sure." Lana gave her a reassuring look. "We were going to make cookies."

"Ryan told us that. They are so excited. It might be because they think they'll be eating cookies as well as making them."

"They're right. You can hardly not taste them to be sure they're okay, right?"

They chuckled together. Then Lana grew serious and her voice dropped. "Thank you for whatever it is that you've done to Ryan. I was worried about him after he quit the rodeo. I thought our small town might not be exciting enough for him. But ever since you came, there's been a big change in him. He smiles more and he seems like he has his zest for life back, if that makes sense."

"I guess it does." Was she responsible for that? "I'm not sure I can take any credit for that."

"I know you can. I think Ryan always thought you were the one that got away."

"We were mostly just friends." She hadn't thought to ask if Lana knew about Maddie, but she assumed she probably did.

"Sometimes friends make the best spouses." Lana winked, then as the music began to play, she hurried away.

"Don't let my mom scare you away from me. I know she has some stories," Ryan said from her other side.

"I'd like to hear those stories," Dakota said, smiling. "And she wasn't trying to scare me away. She...actually thanked me for whatever it was that I did to you. Which, I honestly wasn't sure what she was talking about."

"I know." Ryan's tone held confidence, but he nodded to an empty pew before she could ask what it was. "Is that pew okay?"

"Sure."

He held her elbow as he guided her to their seat. She slid in, giving him plenty of room, before sitting down.

He sat beside her, close enough to put his arm around her, resting it on the back of the pew. Again she had the feeling of being protected, of belonging and of safety. She smiled to herself, thinking that maybe this was what she'd been led to Strawberry Sands for after all.

Chapter 17

"I have something I want to show you," Ryan said as he walked, hand in hand, with Dakota along the beach.

They'd eaten the picnic lunch he'd pre-pared, and had sat on the sand, talking about everything and anything. Nothing serious, just an easy friendship like they used to enjoy, with comfortable silences and conversation that wasn't stilted or difficult. Dakota was the easiest person to talk to. She was thoughtful and articulate without being a know-it-all. She laughed at his jokes and wasn't afraid to tease him, but gently. Not in an unkind way. And she was just as likely to make fun of herself as she was to prod him.

"Really? Okay," she said, her hand holding to his as her skirt swirled around their legs, blown by the stiff breeze that was common over the lake in the spring.

"I loved the rodeo, but I can't imagine living anywhere else," he said, glad she wasn't peppering him with questions about what he had to show her. She just trusted him, going along with what he was going to do like she knew he wouldn't be taking her somewhere she didn't want to go.

He hoped her trust wasn't misguided.

"I've always loved it here." Her words were a little dreamy. "I hope I can make the store work. I'd hate to have to leave."

The idea of her leaving struck fear into his heart.

"Would you stay if you had a choice?" he asked, knowing that what he was about to do could give her that choice.

They took a few steps, with her looking at the ground as though thinking about his question. He tried not to hold his breath, knowing that whatever she answered, he was going to continue with his plan. He was sure it was what God would have him do, so to resist would be foolish.

"I don't know." Her words were so soft they were almost blown away by the wind. They weren't what he wanted to hear, and his heart sank. He wanted her to want to be with him. But he couldn't make her want that. Could only hope that she would decide that on her own.

Of course, he could be clear about his feelings.

But, he couldn't hold onto her. If he loved her, he had to let her go, allow her to make the choice to stay herself. He couldn't believe how hard that was. He wanted to make her love him, didn't want to take the chance that she might choose something or someone else.

They continued to walk, lost in their own thoughts as the stable where he kept his horses came into sight.

"Oh! You're going to show me the geldings you've been working with!" she exclaimed, like they'd never lapsed into silence, or that she'd ever thought about leaving.

"Yeah. And something else." He tried to infuse excitement into his voice.

"Something else?" she repeated, sounding perplexed.

"Yeah. Something I'm going to give you."

"Give me?"

"Hmm. You'd think there were mountains around here with the way your throwing my words back at me."

"You're saying crazy things. What could you possibly have to give me here?"

He just smiled, waiting. The geldings were in the near pasture, and Goldie was on the other side of the barn. She'd be visible in just a few more steps.

It took Dakota a bit, because her experienced eye was taking in his geldings, and she whistled low. "Those fellas are nice."

"They've got great personalities, too," he said, knowing he should be modest, but also knowing that what he said was completely true.

He could see Goldie around the corner of the barn. Maybe she sensed Dakota's presence, because she whinnied, putting her head up in the air, sniffing, before throwing her tail up and galloping forward, like she was running to meet an old, beloved friend. Which she was.

"Goldie?" Dakota said, soft and low, disbelief in her voice. A few heartbeats passed. "That's Goldie, my horse!"

"Yeah."

"I mean, she used to be my horse."

"No. She's still yours."

"How? No. Wait. What?"

"I bought her. But I haven't transferred the papers. And I'm not going to. She's yours."

"You bought her? From me?"

"Yeah. I didn't handle the details because I was working on the store, but yeah."

"I had a friend do the sale for me since my gram had passed..."

"I know."

She turned slowly to look at him. "You've had her since I sold her?"

"Yeah. I couldn't read your name on the contract. And I hadn't had time to look at the papers. But, yeah. And I can't keep her. She belongs to you."

They made it to the fence, where Goldie stretched her head over, reaching for Dakota. With tears in her eyes, Dakota walked under her neck, putting her arms around it and hugging her horse, burying her head in her mane. Horse and woman stood like that for long moments.

Ryan watched, knowing for sure he'd done the right thing. It would set his plans back - he'd need another foundation mare to start his herd with, and he'd need to spend more time saving in order to start the ranch he wanted to, but it was the right thing to do, and to see the two of them together again, it was worth it all.

Finally, after what seemed like a long time, Dakota lifted her head. Goldie nuzzled her neck, making her laugh softly.

"I didn't think I'd ever see her again. It's such a relief to know she's in such good hands."

"Maybe you didn't understand. She's not mine. She's yours."

"I can't take her."

"You can. I insist."

"I don't have any place to keep her."

"I'll keep her until you can."

"It might be years."

"As long as it takes."

She pursed her lips, and pulled back away from her horse, her hands still stroking the golden head. "Why are you doing this?"

He ran a hand through his hair. "I'm not doing it to get any brownie points. Just wanted to be clear about that."

"Okay. That's clear."

Did she sound disappointed? He couldn't be sure.

"You gave up a lot in order for me to win the championships. You kept our daughter-"

"Which I shouldn't have. I should have told you."

"But you did it so that I could do what I'd always dreamed of doing."

She didn't argue.

"It was a sacrifice I didn't deserve. I'm not rich, not by any means, but everything I have now, I have because of you wanting the best for me. Doing what you could to make sure I had every opportunity to be successful. How can I not return that if I can?"

She opened her mouth, but he held up a hand.

"But it's not just because I think I owe you."

"I hope not!" Her words were fervent.

That made him smile.

"It's also because…You said yesterday that love doesn't mean anything unless your actions show it. This might not be the best way to show it, but you and Goldie belong together. If I can make sure that happens, I will. Just…because I love you. And, honestly, I think I always have. Even when we were just friends. That night…that night we had together wouldn't have happened if I hadn't been in love with you already. I guess the alcohol made me less worried about losing our friendship. Even though I regret that sin, I…I loved that night."

An image of Dakota, her eyes closed, a small smile on her face, her hair spread over the pillow as their hands twined together and he leaned over her to kiss her forehead slipped into his head. His throat closed at the feeling that swept through him. Longing for her to be his, not just for a drunken night, but for for-ever.

But he'd told her he loved her and she hadn't had any reaction other than to turn away from him and put her fore-head on her horse's broad head.

He swallowed. He could handle it if she didn't feel the same. If she tried to let him down easy. But not if she chose to cut him out of her life completely. Surely she wouldn't. Not with Maddie in the picture.

"Ryan?" she said, as she let go of her horse and turned toward him.

"Yeah?" His heart lodged in his throat as he waited. The seconds ticked by, feeling like each one contained a year's worth of worry and care.

"I love you, too. I think I always have. How could I not after what you've done for my girls, wanting them both, and for me, fixing my store, making me smile."

He opened his mouth, but it was her turn to put her hand up.

"But it's not just that. I love your character and your desire to do right. To see that Rachel needed a dad as much as

Maddie did and being willing to step in and fill that role. Not just willing, but asking if you could. Your integrity and your willingness to sacrifice to do something kind for me." Her lip trembled a bit. "You make me feel safe."

"You are safe. With me."

"I know. I know you would never hurt me. Not on purpose."

His heart jumped.

"That's the truth. I wish things had turned out differently eight years ago, but I'm hoping you'll give me the chance to make it up to you."

"And me to you. It wasn't all you."

"But I want to take the responsibility for everything. I want to protect you and care for you and cherish you like you deserve." He wanted that with everything in him.

"I keep thinking you're too good to be true."

"Maybe God has just taught me to be a little wiser than I used to be."

She moved from her horse, and he put his hands on her shoulders, sliding them around her back and pulling her toward him.

"If I had to choose between you and Goldie...I'd choose you."

He chuckled a bit. "Some men might not understand that for the major compliment it is."

"That's why I love you. Because you do understand."

"And I love you for it," he murmured as his head lowered and he touched his lips to the side of her head. "I didn't give you the horse to get you to kiss me."

"I didn't think you did. That's too small of a return on your investment."

"A kiss from you is worth more than all the horses in the world."

"I disagree, but I'm happy to kiss you anyway."

And he was happy to take her up on that, moving his head until their lips met and their bodies pressed together and she felt the same, but different, if that was possible. All the feelings burst open in his chest and he kissed her until they were both breathless and clung to each other as he pulled back.

"Kissing you is dangerous." His words were a little wobbly, a little husky, but absolutely true.

"Kissing you is very, very nice," she replied, as wobbly as he, but smiling as big as he'd ever seen her smile.

"I'm not asking you to marry me today, but I'm going to soon."

"Are you warning me so I can grab my horse and run?"

"No. I'm telling you what my intentions are, so you're not surprised."

Her fingers slid down the back of his neck and he was tempted to lower his head again.

"I'll be prepared with my answer, then," she said, a little coyly, but with a sweet smile that turned his heart into a puddle of mush.

"Good to know," he said, giving into the temptation to kiss her again. The first kiss of their rest of their lives. The future wouldn't be without problems, but after the big mistakes they'd made, they'd gotten wiser and would face those problems with the wisdom that came from knowing God had them in the palm of His hand.

Epilogue

Sally bit her lip, trying to focus on the spreadsheet filled with numbers in front of her.

Ever since the barn dance debacle where she'd kidnapped the wrong man, and trapped her best friend and an almost total stranger together in a remote shack in a Michigan snow storm, she'd taken the advice of almost everyone in town and had gotten a job that got her out of her care-giving role for twenty hours a week.

Of course, since her aunt had passed away, she was now looking to increase those hours. Preferably something that had to do with numbers. She loved the regimented flow of spreadsheets, the dependability and the way all the numbers always followed the rules. It was a source of pride to have her ledgers balance each and every time.

Unfortunately, balancing a spreadsheet didn't ease the ache in her heart when she went home alone, ate supper alone, and went to bed, alone.

"Good morning, Sally!"

Dakota Estenben, soon to be Dakota Landry, walked into the inn.

"Good morning! It's going to be another beautiful day!" She didn't have to pretend to be happy for Dakota. She and Ryan made the cutest couple.

"It is." Dakota held up her ring finger. "Ryan proposed last night and I said yes!"

Sally squealed and jumped up, hurrying out from behind her desk and grabbing Dakota's hand so she could peer closer at her ring. "Congratulations! I'm so happy for you!"

"I'm over the moon." Dakota's smile indicated that her words were absolutely true.

"Have you set a date?"

"We'd like to do it soon. That's why I'm here. I was hoping we could rent the kitchen so Griff can cook and we could get married in the courtyard."

"Oh, I think that's totally doable. Franklin and Noah are in their offices, and I'm sure they'll talk to you right now. Go on back the hall - their secretary is at the desk between their doors."

Dakota walked away, and Sally watched her go, happy as she could be for her friend, but the longing in her heart a little deeper and sharper. Seeing other people happy together made her alone-ness feel so much...more.

But if God had someone for her, He'd been doing a good job of keeping the information from her, and until God brought a man for her, she wasn't going to move an inch. As hard as the loneliness was, she would much rather be alone than with the wrong man. She'd seen enough unhappy marriages over the years to know that.

Slowly she walked back around her desk and sat down in front of her computer. Until the man God had for her showed up, she'd take comfort in the perfection of her numbers. She just hoped that wasn't all God had for her. But if it was, she'd try her best to be happy anyway.

Enjoy this preview of There I Find Happiness, just for you!

Chapter 1

"Do you think he's looking at me?"

Sally looked over to where her friend, Norma Jean, indicated.

Peter Slessing stood on the sidewalk outside of the diner in Strawberry Sands, lifting his face to the wind and gazing out on the beautiful blue waters of Lake Michigan.

"I can't tell," Sally said sincerely from where she stood, two steps up on the ladder, hooking a string of lights to a post.

She and Norma Jean were helping to decorate for the Beach Bash that Strawberry Sands was putting on to celebrate the end of summer.

Not that Strawberry Sands really was happy about the end of summer. Since it meant the end of tourist season and the end of good business and lots of tourist dollars.

Although the town would be much quieter from here on out, and Sally wasn't upset about that.

At her job as an accountant at the inn on the edge of town, things would definitely be slowing down. She already didn't have as many hours as what she need-ed since her Aunt Wilma had passed away and she lost her caregiving job. Not that she'd only cared for her Aunt Wilma for the money. She'd loved the lady. Al-though Sally had gotten a little crazy there for a bit when she'd been stuck inside doing nothing but taking care of her twenty-four hours a day, seven days a week.

She'd done one of the silliest things she'd ever done in her life during that time, and it involved her best friend, Norma Jean.

"I think he is. I think he might be coming this way!" Norma Jean's voice contained thrilled excitement.

Ever since Sally had tried to set Norma Jean and Peter up, Norma Jean had been infatuated with the man.

Peter seemed, if not oblivious, only casually interested, and not the kind of interest that made a man propose marriage.

But Sally could never tell Norma Jean that, because Norma Jean was more than just casually interested. She was obsessed with Peter.

"How's my hair look? I wore this shirt because I thought it made my eyes look more blue, but...does it make me look sallow?" Norma Jean's voice held an edge of panic, and Sally tried to infuse calmness into hers.

"You look amazing. As you always do."

Norma Jean had been blessed with beautiful looks, golden hair that flowed in perfect waves past the middle of her back, along with sultry blue eyes and a perfect bone structure.

She was curvy in all the right places, and she turned more than a few heads.

Unfortunately, her personality didn't always match her looks.

"Quick! Get down!"

"From the ladder?" Sally said, confused.

"Yes!" Norma Jean tugged on Sally's shirt, pulling her down and almost making her lose her balance.

"I'm coming," Sally said, somehow allowing Norma Jean's panic to infuse into her own voice. "What's the matter?"

"I need it! If I get up, I can accidentally fall as soon as Peter walks by. Hurry up. I can't fall if you don't move! And if we don't hurry, he'll know we switched on purpose."

He was probably already going to know. The man was less than fifty feet from them, and he would need to walk by if he continued to follow the sidewalk to the sand.

The party was at the edge of town, and the people of Strawberry Sands had been working for days. All of it had been headed up by Eleanor, Sally's friend who had done such a great job on the first annual barn dance last Christmas.

That had been such a raging success that the town had decided to do something like that for the tourists who came every summer.

They hadn't gotten organized in time to do it during the summer, so they decided to celebrate the end of summer.

They were expecting a huge turnout and were hoping to make a good bit of money off of it, enough to hopefully tide everyone over until the next tourist season.

Money might have been the first consideration, but the town wanted everyone to have a good time as well.

And they were pulling out all the stops. They had some big donations, and the decorations were fantastic. The food would be top-notch too, since Griff, who cooked at the diner and owned it with his wife, would be making most of it.

In fact, once Sally was done hanging these lights, she and Norma Jean had planned to stop in at the diner to taste his strawberry cream cheese cobbler. He'd already made three different versions of it, each one better than the last, and Sally could only imagine what this latest version tasted like. If there was any left when she got there.

And if Norma Jean didn't break something when she was trying to fall off the ladder.

"Do you think this is a good idea?" Sally said as Norma Jean scurried up the ladder, the high-heeled sandals she wore making her wobble dangerously.

"Of course! He's barely looked at me since the barn dance. I've got to do something to catch his attention." She looked over the crowd, her eyes searching until they landed on Peter.

Sally opened her mouth, but Norma Jean hissed, "Be quiet! I don't want him to know that we planned this. Not until later. Then I'll tell him, and he'll be amazed at the great lengths I'll go to grab his attention. It will impress him, and we'll tell that story to our great-great-grandchildren."

Sally closed her mouth and held on to the ladder, praying Norma Jean didn't hurt herself.

Also, she was thankful that people's thoughts didn't actually get written in a bubble above their head. If they did, Peter would probably be running in the opposite direction the second he realized that Norma Jean not only had them married but had them pegged as great-great-grandparents.

Sally didn't know a whole lot about men, but she was pretty sure that would be enough to scare almost anyone off. Actually, if some man looked at her and thought about their grandchildren, it would scare her.

Regardless, Norma Jean seemed oblivious to that type of thing. Maybe it was because she was so focused on herself, Sally wasn't sure, but they'd been friends since kindergarten, and Sally loved her, even if she wasn't the easiest person in the world to get along with most of the time.

"All right. Get ready to catch me. I don't actually want to get hurt," Norma Jean hissed, and her voice must have been loud enough to carry to the unsuspecting Peter, since he turned his head and tilted it a little, a friendly smile on his face, only his eyes weren't focused on Norma Jean. He was looking at Sally.

Peter was rather handsome, and she'd had a couple conversations with him. She definitely liked him and would have been interested in him herself, if it hadn't been for Norma Jean.

Well, that and the fact that Peter owned a farm outside of Strawberry Sands, and Sally wasn't exactly farm girl material.

She was an accountant, and she loved her job. She'd quit her job in Chicago in order to care for her Aunt Wilma, but sitting inside, manipulating numbers, drooling over spreadsheets, and creating her own formulas was her idea of a good time.

Not looking at the back end of a cow and dodging the stuff that came out of it.

Of course, Norma Jean didn't exactly seem like that kind of girl either, but that was none of Sally's business. If Peter wanted to choose someone like Norma Jean as a wife, she supposed it would be his responsibility to train her in whatever duties she would be expected to perform on the farm.

Norma Jean probably hadn't thought that far ahead, and Sally hadn't wanted to say anything to destroy the castles that Norma Jean had built in the air, all around Peter. Reality would come crashing in soon enough.

"Peter! Oh, yoohoo, Peter!" Norma Jean's shrill voice seemed to carry over the crowd and be amplified.

Peter's friendly smile wobbled a bit as his eyes shifted from Sally up to Norma Jean. He grimaced as his eyes widened, and later, Sally apologized profusely to Norma Jean because she was so busy looking at the stubble on Peter's jaw and the angled line of his nose that she forgot that she was supposed to have her arms out ready to catch her best friend as she fell off.

She only remembered as Norma Jean tumbled down on top of her, and they both fell to the ground. At least Sally did her job a little, by cushioning Norma Jean's fall.

Unfortunately, she sprained her own ankle in the process, as sharp pain shot up her leg, and her eyes flashed red and black.

"Oh," she groaned.

"You were supposed to catch me!" Norma Jean hissed at her before she turned to Peter with one arm held out. "Oh, Peter, could you please help me. I'm afraid I might have hurt myself," she said, in a completely different tone than the one that she had just used on Sally.

In the meantime, Sally bit back another groan. She didn't want to take Peter's attention off Norma Jean and put it on her. Norma Jean would be furious with her, if Peter ended up helping Sally because Sally hadn't been paying attention and allowed Norma Jean to fall and actually got hurt herself.

She could only imagine Norma Jean's reaction to that.

So she swallowed the groan and winced as Norma Jean's elbow dug into her ribs as she angled herself to reach out to Peter.

"Sally. It looks like your foot bent awkwardly underneath you. Are you okay?"

"I'm fine," Sally said, trying to keep her voice steady and not allow the pain she felt to come out in her tone.

"Peter. What about me? Didn't you see my foot twist awkwardly?" Norma Jean said, waving the hand that Peter still had not grasped.

"No. I missed it." Peter grabbed a hold of her hand and yanked up. In Sally's estimation, he didn't do it very gently but not as hard as what Norma Jean seemed to indicate, as she stumbled forward and crashed into his chest, her arms somehow going around him as she smashed the rest of herself up against him.

"Oh my goodness. I think I did twist my ankle just slightly. I don't seem to be able to put any weight on it. At all," Norma Jean said as one hand trailed down Peter's cheek and the other continued to hold tightly to him, while she kept her right foot held up in the air as though it hurt.

"That's funny. You landed on your left side. I would have thought that would have been the foot that hurt," Peter said as he held his hands up in the air, as though he wasn't sure what to do with them. His chin picked up several notches, but he seemed to be gazing down over his nose at Sally and not Norma Jean. At least, that's what it looked like when she glanced up. She only did it for a second, because she had to focus on rolling over, putting both hands on the ground, and pulling her good leg under-neath her.

She grabbed the rung of the ladder and started to push up.

"Are you okay? Can I give you a hand?" Peter said as she continued to try to pull herself to her feet, and Norma Jean con-tinued to press herself against him.

Normally Peter was known as jovial and goofy, but he seemed rather serious to-day. Or maybe it was because he wasn't used to having two women falling at his feet in front of him, and it scared him.

Sally snorted, even though the pain from her ankle pressed up her leg and out both elbows.

"Thank you. I... I just thought it'd be fun to lean on the ladder and make sure that it was still sturdy. I don't want someone to get hurt and it to be our fault."

She couldn't think of any other excuse off the top of her head for why she would be slowly using her hands to climb up the ladder while not using one foot.

"You're not putting any weight on that foot. Why not?"

"I often enjoy hopping around on one leg. I find it...helps me balance when I'm on ladders in the air," Sally said, feeling stupid, because she wasn't good at making up stories on the spot. She'd never been a great liar, and this felt dangerously close to being not only a lie but a completely unbelievable lie, which were the worst kind of lie. Although, Norma Jean had often coached her to tell the most outrageous lie she could possibly think of and then just pretend it was true.

"Oh, Peter. Oh my goodness. I think I... I feel faint. Could you help me over to that bench, please?"

The newly installed benches lined the sidewalk up and down the street of Strawberry Sands. They were a great addition, as were the shade trees that had been planted near each bench.

They were just saplings, but someone with a lot of foresight had taken the first steps that would make downtown

Strawberry Sands a beautiful place to be, in ten or fifteen years.

Not that it wasn't now, but it certainly would be even more wonderful once the trees had grown up.

"I'm pretty sure you were limping on your right leg before. But now it's your left."

"That's because you said I landed on my left side, so it must have been my left foot that got hurt!" Norma Jean said, stomping her foot on the ground. Her left foot.

"You walked on both of them with no problem. I think you're fine."

"I'm not fine. That's exactly what I've been trying to tell you!" Norma Jean draped herself over Peter, with one arm behind him, one arm gripping his front, while she again hopped on her left foot, holding her right foot in the air.

"Let me help you over," Peter finally said, walking toward the bench and bending down so she dropped on it with a plop.

Her hands must have become untangled, and Peter jumped back.

"Let me see to your friend, and I'll be back."

By this time, Sally had gotten up and stood, still gripping the ladder.

She tried putting a little weight on her right foot, but the pain had gotten so bad she was afraid she was going to black out. So she lifted it up immediately.

But now, with Peter walking toward her, she kept both legs so the bottoms of her feet touched the ground, even though she wasn't putting any weight on her right foot.

Hopefully she could fake it until she made it. That should keep Norma Jean from being upset with her.

"I'm fine. You can take care of Norma Jean. I... I was just going to stand here and enjoy the view for a little bit."

"Once you walk on that foot."

"I will. I'll walk on it a lot. In fact, I think I might run up to the diner. I was excited about the strawberry cream cheese cobbler, and that's enough to make anyone run. Even though I'm not normally a runner." Sally clamped her mouth shut. She had a tendency to ramble on when she shouldn't.

But she also had a tendency to be nice to the point of being what Norma Jean called a doormat. She didn't really see a problem with being nice. She saw more of a problem with taking advantage of people who were nice. But that wasn't her area. Her area was just to be kind, since that's what God's command was. And she wasn't commanded to police anyone who wasn't following what the Bible said.

"I'm not normally a runner either, but I feel the same way about strawberry cream cheese cobbler. Would you be interested—"

"Oh my goodness. Look at the time. Norma Jean!" Sally said, interrupting Peter who seemed to be on the verge of asking her to head to the diner and eat with him. Norma Jean would go ballistic if she heard that. Especially when she was over there waiting for Peter to get back to her. She'd never talk to Sally again.

"Norma Jean! Didn't you say that you had to be down at the band practice at twelve o'clock?"

"No. It was one thirty," Norma Jean said, scrunching up her face like she was thinking about it.

"No. I'm sure you said it was twelve o'clock," Sally said, trying to look around

Peter to give that look to Norma Jean. The look that said if she wanted to go with Peter, she needed to pretend to need to get to band practice. Sally wasn't very good at that look. She wasn't very good at subtlety at all. She was much more of a straightforward, I'll just be nice to everyone, I don't want to make any waves, I'd rather be kind, kind of person.

"Oh!" Norma Jean said, jumping up, running over, and grabbing onto Peter's arm. "I totally forgot about that. Oh, Peter, I need you to help me walk to the grandstand where the band is practicing. Please. I don't want to be late."

"I don't see anyone over at the grandstand." Peter gave Sally a look, and Sally thought that maybe he seemed a little disappointed.

Disappointed because she was friends with Norma Jean? Or disappointed because he had hoped to go to the diner with her?

She wasn't sure. And she had to dismiss it. There was no way she could have anything to do with Peter while she and Norma Jean were friends and Norma Jean was infatuated with him.

She wouldn't do that to her friend. Peter was off-limits to her.

"Please. Can you please help me walk over? I just don't think I can do it on my own," Norma Jean said as she slipped her arm around Peter's waist and started to limp toward the grandstand. Peter had no choice but to follow along with her, steadying her.

"I'd appreciate it if you take care of that foot. Get it looked at," Peter said over his shoulder.

Sally nodded, not looking at his face, but rather her eyes were caught on the hand that hung at his waist. It was big and brown, with long fingers, a hand that knew how to work.

She liked that kind of hand.

But she stared at it for a few moments before she remembered what she'd just thought. Peter was off-limits to her.

Pick up your copy of There I Find Happiness by Jessie Gussman today!

wsletter – I laughed so hard I sprayed it out all over the table!"

Claim your free
book from Jessie!